The Case of the Mellow Maltese

A Thousand Islands Doggy Inn Mystery

B.R. Snow

This book is a work of fiction. Names, characters, places and events are either used fictitiously or are the product of the author's imagination. All rights reserved, including the right to reproduce this book, or portions thereof, in any form. No part of this text may be reproduced, transmitted, downloaded, decompiled, or stored in or introduced into any information storage and retrieval system, in any form by any means, whether electronic or mechanical without the express written consent of the author. The scanning, uploading, and distribution of this book via the Internet or any other means without the permission of the publisher are illegal and punishable by law.

Copyright © 2017 B.R. Snow
ISBN: 978-1-942691-39-6

Website: www.brsnow.net/
Twitter:@BernSnow
Facebook: facebook.com/bernsnow

Cover Design: Reggie Cullen
Cover Photo: James R. Miller

Other Books by B.R. Snow

The Thousand Islands Doggy Inn Mysteries

- The Case of the Abandoned Aussie
- The Case of the Brokenhearted Bulldog
- The Case of the Caged Cockers
- The Case of the Dapper Dandie Dinmont
- The Case of the Eccentric Elkhound
- The Case of the Faithful Frenchie
- The Case of the Graceful Goldens
- The Case of the Hurricane Hounds
- The Case of the Itinerant Ibizan
- The Case of the Jaded Jack Russell
- The Case of the Klutzy King Charles
- The Case of the Lovable Labs

The Whiskey Run Chronicles

- Episode 1 – The Dry Season Approaches
- Episode 2 – Friends and Enemies
- Episode 3 – Let the Games Begin
- Episode 4 – Enter the Revenuer
- Episode 5 – A Changing Landscape
- Episode 6 – Entrepreneurial Spirits
- Episode 7 – All Hands On Deck
- The Whiskey Run Chronicles – The Complete Volume 1

The Damaged Posse

- American Midnight
- Larrikin Gene
- Sneaker World
- Summerman
- The Duplicates

Other Books

- Divorce Hotel
- Either Ore

To Karen and Daisy

Chapter 1

I watched Chef Claire work her way across the surface of the water and shook my head. It was a headshake comprised of two parts; one in amazement, the other in disbelief. I was amazed by how easy she was making her paddleboard journey look. Standing tall and pulling the long paddle she held with both hands through the water, her concentration unbroken despite the streams of sweat pouring down her face and shoulders, the board gliding forward despite the headwind she was fighting. My disbelief stemmed from the still unanswered question of why any sane individual would choose to stand on a piece of fiberglass in the middle of the St. Lawrence and paddle like crazy just to see how fast and far they could travel.

"She's getting good on that thing," Josie said, offering me the bag of bite-sized Snickers.

I grabbed a couple and stretched my legs out on the bench seat that ran across the stern and nodded as I adjusted my sunglasses.

"Yes, she certainly is," I said, popping a bite-sized without taking my eyes off Chef Claire. "But that doesn't mean she hasn't lost her mind."

"I know," Josie said, unwrapping a bite-sized. "If she was older, I might even consider her a bit of a dotard."

"Dotard?"

"An older person who has pretty much lost the plot."

"Really? I've never heard the term before."

"It's been in the news lately," Josie said, tossing back another bite-sized.

"I'm trying to cut back on the amount of news I watch," I said, motioning for her to hold the bag closer. "Every time I do watch it, I always end up thinking that losing the plot might not be a bad way to go."

Josie laughed and made room for her massive Newfie, Captain, who'd decided he wanted to use her lap as a pillow.

"But since Chef Claire is still young, I'm gonna go with nuts."

"It looks brutal," I said, staring out at the water as Chef Claire turned the paddleboard around and headed back toward the boat. "But she's an athlete, and that's the sort of thing athletes do, right?"

2

"Yeah, I'm sure it is. But all the energy she's using probably equals what three people would go through in a workout," Josie said, staring out at her.

"That's a good point," I said, glancing over at Josie. "I'm gonna count it."

"Well, we are *watching* her," Josie said, laughing. "That must burn some calories."

"Exactly."

Chef Claire was training for an event called the 147. It was the brainchild of my mother and her latest project designed to fill one of the late summer weekends with an activity that would attract large numbers of visitors and extend the tourist season a little longer past Labor Day. Ostensibly, it was a triathlon, but all three events would take place on the water and consisted of swimming, paddleboarding, and kayaking. My mother had hit on the idea during one of our Monday night family dinners, and we'd spent the next hour trying to come up with a good name for it. Waterthon, Wet and Wild, SplashFest, and a host of others were discussed then discarded, but we continued our search until Josie had suggested the 147 to designate the distance each of the three events would cover. I thought that a mile swim, a four-mile paddleboard journey through a winding course, followed by a brutal seven-mile kayak trip should be called something more befitting the event and suggested the Insanity Invitational, but I got outvoted.

But Chef Claire had immediately announced her intention of participating, and Josie and I had laughed and laughed and laughed until Chef Claire whacked both of us on the hand with a wooden spoon. Now, with the event two-days away, we were once again out on our boat supervising her training.

Our term, not hers.

She approached the boat, and all four of our dogs hopped up onto the bow and barked to welcome her. She straddled the board and held onto the boat with one hand as she tried to catch her breath. Sweat poured down her entire body, and the muscles in her shoulders were twitching from the workout. I handed her a bottle of water, and she gulped it down in two large swallows. She tossed the empty bottle onto the boat then slid into the water and lifted the end of her paddleboard. Josie and I pulled it onboard then helped Chef Claire into the boat. The dogs greeted her, and she petted all of them, then leaned back, legs splayed. She glanced down at the tracking device on her wrist and shook her head sadly.

"That was just under four miles," Chef Claire said. "It felt like fifty."

"And you didn't do the swim first," I said, offering her the bag of bite-sized. She waved it away, exhausted.

"Not to mention the seven-mile kayak trip to finish," Josie said.

"What have I gotten myself into?" Chef Claire said, arching her back. "I'm a chef, not a triathlete."

"It's not too late to back out," Josie said, reaching for the bag.

"I'd look like a big baby if I did that," she said, grabbing another bottle of water.

"Fake an injury," I said, shrugging. "That's what I'd do. A pulled hamstring should work."

"You don't even know where your hamstring is," Josie said, laughing.

I made a face at her, then grinned.

"No, I have to go through with it," Chef Claire said. "Just on principle alone."

"Have it your way," Josie said, opening a bottle of wine. "What's the special tonight at the restaurant?"

"We're doing a two for one surf and turf," Chef Claire said, waving off Josie's offer of wine.

"Perfect," Josie said, then glanced at me. "What are you gonna have?"

Chef Claire and I both laughed. But we knew that Josie wasn't kidding. She'd be able to polish off both and still have room for dessert.

"You should be the one on the paddleboard," Chef Claire said. "You know, to work off all those calories."

"Hey, I spend all day dealing with fifty dogs. Trust me, that's all the workout I need."

"I should have thought of that before I signed up for this stupid thing," Chef Claire said, getting to her feet and rubbing her lower back with a grimace.

"Do what I do at times like this," I said.

"What's that?"

"Blame my mother."

"I can't do that," Chef Claire said. "She tried to talk me out of it, too. How many people have signed up to do this thing?"

"Just over two hundred," I said.

"Society continues to lose its collective mind," Josie said as she sat down in the driver seat. "We should get going. Somebody has to work tonight."

"Don't remind me," Chef Claire said, sitting back down. Her Goldens, Al and Dente, hopped up on the seat next to her and she stroked their heads. "Your mama is an idiot. You do know that, don't you?" Both dogs thumped their tails on the padded seat then rolled over onto their backs in unison. Chef Claire used both hands for their tummy rubs.

Josie started the engine, and we were soon cruising across the water heading for home. About five minutes later, I caught a glimpse of something off to our right in the distance, and I put a hand on her shoulder and pointed. Josie pulled back on the throttle and veered right.

"What is that?" she said, squinting into the sunlight that was reflecting off the water.

"I'm not sure," I said. "If I didn't know better, I'd swear it was a paddleboard."

"I don't see anybody on it," Josie said, slowing the boat even further. "But it looks like there's something on it. What's that white thing?"

"Maybe a towel," I said. "No, whatever it is, it's moving."

"Wait a sec," Josie said. "I think it's a dog."

I grabbed my binoculars and focused on the object floating in the distance.

"It's a Maltese," I said, frowning. "What the heck is a dog doing on a paddleboard all by itself in the middle of the River?"

"I have no idea," Josie said, accelerating. "But we are certainly going to find out."

When we got close to the paddleboard and the dog, Josie put the boat in neutral, and we drifted until we were right next to the board. The dog was trembling but didn't appear to be panicked, and when it saw us, the dog got to its feet and wagged its tail. Our dogs stared down at the Maltese, apparently also confused by what they were seeing.

"Weird," Josie said, staring at the Maltese.

"That's the word for it," I said, leaning over the side of the boat.

The dog took a step closer, sniffed my hand, then licked it. I lifted the dog onto the boat and gently set her down on the padded seat next to me.

"We should probably grab the board, too," Josie said, still puzzled. She pulled the paddleboard out of the water and set it down on the deck. "Wow, that's really light."

"Fiberglass," Chef Claire said, shrugging.

Josie and I examined the Maltese who was sitting quietly but closely watching our movements. I examined the collar she was wearing and read the name tag.

"Her name's Mellow," I said, rubbing the dog's head.

"That's a great name for her," Chef Claire said. "Look at that face. It's like she doesn't have a care in the world."

"She must be used to being out here on the board," Josie said, kneeling down to pet the Maltese that was a brilliant white with dark eyes and cute as all get out.

Then the Maltese emitted a soft whimper followed by two barks. Josie rubbed her hand over the dog's back, and she relaxed and licked Josie's hand.

"But where the heck is her owner?" I said, using my binoculars to survey the immediate stretch of water.

"That's a very good question," Josie said, standing up to join me in my search. "You think whoever it was might have gotten into some sort of trouble and fallen in?"

"That's the only thing that makes any sense," I said, frowning as my scan of the water came up empty. "But if they did fall in, wouldn't the board have tipped over? The dog is dry as a bone."

"Maybe she fell in a couple of hours ago, and she dried off," Chef Claire said, shrugging.

"I suppose," I said. "I don't have a good feeling about this. This is too bizarre."

I grabbed my phone and made the call. Chief Abrams answered on the third ring, and I set the phone down on the seat and put it on speaker.

"Hey, Snoopmeister," the Chief said. "I thought you guys were going out on the River to watch Chef Claire torture herself."

"We did," I said. "And mission accomplished."

"Hey, at least I'm making an effort," Chef Claire said, shooting me a dirty look.

"Actually, we're still out here. We're near the entrance to the Lake of the Isles," I said, returning Chef Claire's glare with a grin.

"And since it's such a beautiful day over there, you're calling just to rub it in?" the Chief said.

"No, we found something you probably want to check out."

"Not another one?" the Chief said, his voice rising. "What is it with you and dead bodies?"

"No, it's not that," I said, glancing around the water again. "At least, not yet. We found a dog sitting on a paddleboard all by itself in the middle of the River."

"Okay," he said. "You have my attention."

"She's a gorgeous Maltese," I said. "But we don't have a clue how she ended up out here all by herself."

"And you think that something bad might have happened to her owner?"

"Nothing gets past you, Chief."

"Don't get smart with me, *young lady*," he said, doing his best imitation of my mother.

"Not bad. You've almost got it," I said, laughing. "But the thought that something bad might have happened did cross our minds."

"Okay, I'll grab the police boat and head over. Can you guys stick around until I get there?"

I glanced at my watch then at Chef Claire. She checked her own watch then nodded.

"I'm good," she said. "I was planning on taking a shower first, but I'll just head straight to the restaurant when we get back."

"We'll be here," I said. "You'll see us a couple hundred yards on your left as soon as you make the turn into the lake."

"Okay. Is the dog hurt? You need me to bring anything?"

"No," I said, rubbing the Maltese's head. "Actually, she's doing remarkably well."

"I would have thought the dog would be freaked out," the Chief said. "Too bad she can't talk, right?"

"Oh, she's talking. It's just that we can't understand a word she's saying."

Chapter 2

I put my knife and fork down then swiveled on my stool and glanced around the crowded lounge. Still surprised by the number of people in the restaurant, I turned back to the bar and watched Josie who was in the final stages of making her second lobster tail disappear. Millie, our head bartender, although well-versed in Josie's prodigious appetite, still shook her head then caught my eye.

"Can I take your plate without running the risk of getting stabbed with a fork?" Millie deadpanned.

"Funny," Josie said, wiping her mouth. "I'll swap you. The plate for a dessert menu."

I snorted then reached for my wine glass.

"Your mother certainly knows what she's doing," Millie said, nodding at the crowd. "This looks more like a night in July than September."

"Yeah, we'll probably do over two hundred dinners," I said. "Chef Claire will sleep good tonight."

"I still can't believe she entered that thing," Millie said. "It's…how do I even describe it?"

"Self-inflicted torture," Josie said, not looking up from the dessert menu.

"Close enough," Millie said.

"No desire to get out on the water and join the fun?" I said.

"Yeah, right," Millie said, scoffing. "I spent all afternoon bench-pressing cases of beer and wine. That's all the workout I need. How about you, Josie? You going to enter?"

Josie glanced up and raised an eyebrow at Millie who laughed when she saw the expression on her face.

"Maybe your mother will organize a competitive eating contest," Millie said.

"Don't give her any ideas," I said.

"Don't give who any ideas, darling?"

I turned around and smiled at my mother then gave her a hug.

"Hey, Mom. I didn't know you were here," I said, glancing into the packed dining room. "Who are you having dinner with?"

"The people handling the logistics of the 147 and a couple of their sponsors," she said, giving Josie a hug and a kiss on the cheek. "Let me guess, you had the two for one surf and turf."

"As a matter of fact, I did," Josie said. "How'd you know that?"

"Well, unless you've started using it as a body lotion, it's the only way to explain all that butter," my mother said, nodding at the large stain on Josie's blouse.

"Again?" Josie said, glancing down and shaking her head. "I can't believe it." She slid off her barstool. "I'll be right back."

We watched her head for the ladies' room, then my mother slid into Josie's seat.

"Nice crowd," she said, nodding. "I think this might become an annual event."

"I can't believe there are over two hundred people who willingly signed up for it," I said. "Are the folks you're having dinner with nice?"

"They are," my mother said. "And one of the guys at the table is perfect for you, darling. You should stop by, and I'll introduce you. He's *gorgeous*."

"Maybe in a bit," I said, reaching for my wine glass.

My mother shook her head and patted my hand.

"Can I get you anything, Mrs. C.?" Millie said.

"No, I'm good for now, dear. How are you doing, Millie?"

"Really good. I love it here."

Millie had formerly owned and operated a bar in town not far from the restaurant. But after working eighty hours a week for five years, she'd gotten tired of the grind and had sold the place. And when our former bar manager, Rocco, fell in love in Cayman and decided to live there year-round, Millie had offered her services to us. We'd immediately accepted, and the restaurant hadn't missed a beat.

"I'll need to get back soon," my mother said. "But I had to get away for a few minutes. That poor woman is hysterical."

"What's the matter with her?" I said.

"Someone stole her dog," my mother said. "What a despicable thing to do."

My neurons flared, and I stared at my mother. Josie returned from the bathroom with a huge wet spot on the front of her blouse.

"I think I got most of it out," Josie said, glancing down. "I need to start wearing a bib." She noticed the look on my face and frowned. "What did I miss? Did you two have another fight?"

"No, we haven't had time to get to that yet," I said.

"Funny, darling. I was just telling Suzy that one of the women I'm having dinner with had her dog stolen today."

Josie's expression now matched mine. My mother glanced back and forth at us.

"Do you two have something you'd like to tell me?" she said.

"The dog? It isn't a Maltese by any chance, is it?" I said.

"As a matter of fact, it is," my mother said, frowning. "Please tell me you didn't steal that poor woman's dog."

"Geez, Mom. Must you?"

"I'm just checking, darling."

"We have the dog," Josie said. "And she's safe and sound."

Josie spent a few minutes explaining how we happened to come into possession of the Maltese. My mother listened closely then headed into the dining room and soon returned with a woman she introduced as Maria. She looked like she'd been crying for a long time.

"You have Mellow?" she said, obviously relieved by the news my mother had given her.

"We do," I said. "And she's fine. I'm Suzy. And this is Josie."

"Nice to meet you," she said, flashing a quick smile. "Where did you find her?"

"She was on a paddleboard in the middle of the River," I said. "We've got your board, too."

"What?" Maria said, stunned.

"Yeah, that was pretty much our reaction," I said. "We took a look to see if anybody was around then called the chief of police. He also searched the immediate area but didn't find anything. Has anyone gone missing from your group?"

"No," Maria said, frowning. "And you say that Mellow was just sitting on the board?"

"Yes, and she was totally relaxed when we found her," Josie said. "She's obviously well-named."

"Mellow is very used to being on the board," Maria said. "I take her out with me all the time. But how the heck did she end up out there all by herself?"

"That seems to be the question of the moment," I said, shrugging. "But I can't believe anybody would do that on purpose."

"Yes, well, I guess we'll see about that," Maria said, her eyes narrowing. "Would it be possible to go get her?"

"Absolutely," I said.

"I'll take you," Josie said, reaching into her bag for her car keys. "I need to change my blouse."

"Okay," I said, nodding. "You want me to order you a soufflé? It should be just about ready by the time you get back."

"You read my mind," Josie said, then looked at Maria. "Are you ready to go?"

"I'm more than ready," she said.

We watched them leave through the front door, then I settled back into my seat with a frown.

"What's the matter, darling?"

"Her comment about I guess we'll see about that," I said. "It sounded like she had somebody in mind."

"Darling, nobody's dead. So, just take a breath."

Millie laughed then headed off to fill a drink order.

"It was a weird comment, Mom. But you're right, it's probably nothing."

"That's my girl," she said, patting my hand. "Now, how about you follow me into the dining room and let me introduce you."

"What does he do for a living?"

"He's an executive with the brewery that's sponsoring the 147. In public relations."

"So, he's a beer salesman."

"No, he's not a beer salesman," my mother said, glaring at me. "I know what you're doing."

"What am I doing, Mom?"

"Putting up a barrier before you've even met the man. You always do that every time I try to introduce you to someone."

"Well, given your track record with fix-ups, you can't really blame me," I said, deciding to poke the bear.

"I see," she said, annoyed. "So, you don't want to meet him?"

"Maybe later," I said, smiling at her. "How about you introduce me to him at the race?"

"Do you want to run the risk of waiting? He might be off the market in a few days."

"I'll take my chances, Mom."

"You're impossible," she said, chewing on her bottom lip. Then she spotted Millie returning. "Millie, would you please try talking some sense into my daughter?"

"Sure," Millie deadpanned, then stared at me. "Suzy?"

"Yeah?"

"Listen to your mother."

I glanced up at her, smiled, then took a gulp of wine. Millie shrugged her shoulders at my mother.

"I gave it a shot."

"Why do I even bother?" my mother said, then headed back into the dining room.

"Well played," I said, raising my glass in a toast.

"No problem. But you might want to reconsider," Millie said. "I just got a look at the guy she's trying to fix you up with. He's smoking."

"I assume you're not talking about cigarettes."

"Nothing gets past you."

Millie gave me a finger-wave as she again headed off to fill another drink order. I ordered two chocolate soufflés from one of the servers then spent the next fifteen minutes sitting at the bar catching up with a few friends I hadn't seen for a while. Josie strolled in wearing a different blouse and sat down next to me. This one was light blue with an abstract black and white pattern that caught my attention immediately.

"Is that new?"

"Yeah, your mom got me this for my birthday, remember? At first, I wasn't sure. But she nailed it again."

"Speaking of birthdays, did you get a chance to speak to the breeder?"

"I did," she said. "We'll be able to pick the puppy up sometime next week."

My mother's birthday was coming up soon, and we were giving her a King Charles spaniel puppy. During our recent trip to Grand Cayman, we had crossed paths with a King Charles, and my mother had taken care of the dog until we were able to reunite him with his owner. To say that my mother had bonded with the dog was a major understatement, and she'd had a hard time giving him up.

"Did everything go okay at the Inn?" I said, sliding the glass of wine I'd been keeping an eye on toward her.

"Piece of cake."

"I thought you wanted the soufflé."

"Funny. I called the Inn on my way over, and Michelle had the Maltese ready to go by the time we got there."

"I assume it was a happy reunion," I said.

"She was bouncing up and down, tongue hanging out, and making this adorable happy squeal," Josie said, waving at somebody in the lounge.

"Good. I'm glad to hear that," I said, nodding.

"The dog was pretty happy, too."

I glanced over at her but didn't bother to respond.

"She and her boyfriend have a company that makes paddleboards," Josie said. "And I think she said they also make surfboards and kayaks."

"Really? That's interesting. And they travel around sponsoring events like ours to promote their products?"

"They do," Josie said. "They spend half the year north of the equator, then spend the rest of it in places like Tahiti and Australia."

21

"Not the briar patch," I said, grinning at her.

"Yeah, tell me about it," Josie said. "But they're on the road over forty weeks a year. That's gotta be a grind."

"Still a pretty good way to see the world while you're young enough to enjoy it. Where are they staying while they're here?"

"They rented a place on Wellesley Island near where the 147 is taking place. You know that big A-frame with all the picture windows?"

"Sure. That's the Anderson place," I said. "I think he's been pretty sick, so they've been renting it out the past few summers."

"There's eight of them," Josie said. "And Maria said they're having a barbeque tomorrow night. We've been invited."

"Might be fun," I said, nodding. "Maybe we'll be able to figure out who left the dog on the board."

"You're unbelievable," Josie said.

"Aren't you sweet."

"Just let it go, Suzy."

"Sure, sure. Who are the people staying there?"

"Most of them work for their company, but a couple of their sponsors are also in for the week."

"One of them must be the guy my mother is trying to fix me up with," I said.

"Ah, the dreaded fix-up," Josie said. "What does this one do?"

"He's a beer salesman."

One of the servers arrived carrying our chocolate soufflés and set them down in front of us.

"Here you go, folks," he said. "Enjoy. But be careful, they're very hot."

"Thanks, Jorge," I said, then glanced at Josie. "Did you hear what he said?"

"Yeah, I heard," she said, shaking her head at me as she picked up her spoon. "I have eaten chocolate soufflé before."

"Okay, I'm just saying be careful."

Josie dug in and slid a heaping spoonful of the soufflé into her mouth. Then she gasped and grabbed her napkin. She wiped her mouth, then took a long drink of water.

"Hot," she said, her eyes watering.

"Thanks for the warning," I said, laughing.

Josie made a face at me, then dipped her spoon into the soufflé again. She spent several seconds blowing on it then raised the spoon to her mouth. She blew on it one final time, and the soufflé slid off the spoon and landed with a soft plop on her blouse.

"Are you freaking kidding me?"

"Try taking human bites."

Chapter 3

I slowed down as I approached the long dock that fronted the impressive stone and glass A-frame that dominated the shoreline and was set against the backdrop of a gorgeous sunset dominated by red and orange. Josie hopped out of the boat and tied it off then glanced around at the property as she waited for me to make my way onto the dock.

"Nice," Josie said. "Business must be good. What do you think it costs to rent this for a week?"

"A lot," I said, admiring the house and lawn. "But it's probably still cheaper than hotel rooms for eight people."

"Good point," Josie said, waving to Maria who was heading our way holding the Maltese under one arm.

"I'm so glad you could come," Maria said. "Your friend, Chef Claire, couldn't make it?"

"No, she's working tonight," Josie said, reaching out to rub the Maltese's head. "Then she's going straight home to bed. She says she's going to need every bit of energy to make it through tomorrow."

"I'm sure she'll do fine," Maria said. "Why didn't you two enter?"

25

Josie snorted.

"You're new here, right?" I said, laughing. "We'll be more than happy as interested spectators."

"Come on up to the house and meet everyone," Maria said. "Are you guys hungry?"

"Trick question, right?" Josie whispered as we followed her to the end of the dock and up the stone path.

Maria led us up onto the deck that wrapped around the house. Everyone glanced up to give us the once-over as we approached, and we sat down in two of the Adirondack chairs that were arranged in a circle not far from the grill. The smells, apart from the unmistakable scent of salmon, were incredible and I felt my stomach gurgle. Maria handled the introductions starting with the man whose lap she was now stretched out on.

"Suzy, Josie, this is Julian, CEO of Paddles, and the love of my life," Maria said, nuzzling her boyfriend's neck.

He gave us a goofy grin, and judging by the glazed look in his eyes, I assumed he'd started drinking rather early in the day.

"It's nice to meet you," Julian said. "I'd try to shake hands, but I don't think that's going to be possible at the moment."

"Don't worry about it," I said, smiling. "It's the thought that counts."

"On our right, are Rock and Kirk, two of the best board designers you could ever hope to find," Maria said.

"Hi," I said, nodding at both of them. "You design all the paddleboards?"

"We do," Rock said. "And the surfboards and kayaks. But Kirk here is the real guru."

"Nice to meet you," Kirk said, his eyelids half-shut.

Both of them had long, bleached hair and fit the stereotype of the surfer-beach bum. Whether or not the hair was the result of the sun or had come from a bottle was unclear, but the look worked for them.

"Next to you are Layla and Kim," Maria said. "They handle sales and marketing. And they both do *amazing* jobs."

They both gave us small waves then refocused on what appeared to be margaritas.

"Layla? Like the song?" Josie said.

"Yes," Layla said, nodding over the top of her glass. "I think my parents got most of their inspiration from album covers back in the day."

"And next to them is Emma," Maria said. "She's one of our corporate sponsors. She works for Wet Water Fashions."

"Oh, I love your stuff," Josie said. "I've got half a closet of your tops alone."

"As someone who gets bonused on company sales, I salute you," she said, raising her glass in a toast.

"And next to Emma is Matisse, senior vice president of public relations for Cervisial Breweries."

"It's nice to meet you, Matisse," I said, feeling my face flush. Millie and my mother hadn't been kidding. I flinched and exhaled softly, and he also got a whispered grunt out of Josie. He grinned at both of us, and I brushed my hair away from my face and made a mental note to apologize to my mother and clear my calendar for the next few days.

"Matisse," Josie said. "That's a French name, right?"

"Close enough, if you believe the Francophiles north of the border. I'm from Montreal."

"Loosely translated, your name means God's gift," Josie said.

"Yes, so I've been told," Matisse said with a smug grin.

Josie leaned closer toward me.

"Geez, why do they always have to ruin it by talking?" Josie whispered.

"Yeah, I know," I said, whispering back. "Oh, well, it was fun while it lasted."

Josie laughed, then flushed red with embarrassment.

"Did I miss something?" Matisse said, cocking his head at us.

"Oh, Suzy was just telling me a funny story about her back," Josie said, immediately recovering. "It was cramping up on the ride over."

"Yeah, it's been acting up," I said, lying through my teeth. "I've spent the past few days flat on my back."

"I see," Matisse said, staring at me, then looking over at Kirk, the surfboard designer. "Je voudrais l'avoir sur le dos." Then he gave me a look that could only be described as a creepy leer. If he'd been wearing a raincoat and hanging around the park, I would have had him arrested.

"Il faudrait queue tu me tire d'abord," I said with a cold stare.

Matisse flinched and started picking at the label on his beer bottle.

"Oh, you speak French," Matisse said.

"Rien ne vous dépasse," I snapped.

"I think we missed something," Maria said, glancing back and forth at us.

"Matisse was just saying how much he'd like to get Suzy on her back," Josie said, glaring at him.

"Really, Matisse?" Maria said, shaking her head. "They've been here two minutes, and you've already insulted our guests. Why do you always insist on proving what a jerk you can be?" She focused on me. "I'm so sorry, Suzy."

"Don't worry about it," I said, shrugging.

"What was your comeback? It certainly shut him up."

"I told him he'd have to shoot me first."

Everyone, with the exception of Matisse, laughed long and hard. Matisse drained the last of his beer and headed for a cooler to grab a fresh one.

"Let's head inside, and I'll get you guys something to drink," Maria said, climbing off her boyfriend's lap. "And then we'll eat."

I followed everyone inside and looked around the massive open space that dominated the first floor. The ceiling was at least fifty feet high, and the combination of stone, glass, and wood looked like it had come straight out of an interior design magazine. Maria returned from the kitchen area holding two glasses of wine and handed them to us. She gestured for us to take a seat at the long dining room table that was already filled with several covered platters, and I sat down between her and Josie. Matisse was sitting on the other side of the table between the two board designers, still pouting and licking his wounds.

"Thanks again for rescuing Mellow," Maria said, handing me a platter filled with grilled salmon. I passed it along to Josie and waited for the next one.

"Don't mention it," I said, spying a tray of steaks that was heading my way. "Did you figure out what happened yet?"

"The best thing we can come up with is that Mellow headed down to the dock by herself. We've had a bunch of boards sitting near shore. She must have gotten onto one, and it somehow slid into the water. The wind was out of the west yesterday, and it probably blew her and the board out. Mellow is used to being on the board with me, and it probably didn't even faze her. But I'm so lucky you guys happened to be out there to find her. I don't know what I'd do if anything ever happened to her."

Maria paused to take a long sip of wine then glanced over at me. I gave her a small smile. She'd pretty much blurted the entire story out in one breath. As far as cover stories went, it wasn't bad, but I knew instinctively that it was all a lie. The board would have to be in the water, not on shore, for it to end up in the middle of the Lake of the Isles since there was no way a small dog like the Maltese could have pushed the board off the shoreline. And as I knew, along with everyone who had entered the 147, the wind had been blowing hard out of the east for the past several days and was expected to do the same tomorrow, thereby making portions of the paddleboard and kayak events particularly difficult given the headwind the participants would be forced to deal with.

I had no idea why she felt the need to lie to me, but my neurons flared, and my Snoopmeter turned itself on.

"Well, I'm just glad she's okay," I said, patting her hand.

I filled my plate with steak, a piece of chicken, and three different salads. The food was outstanding, and the dinner conversation was casual and focused primarily on the business activities of the company named Paddles. I tried to follow the thread, but as soon as the conversation veered away from the actual products they made into a mind-numbing debate about whether or not they were ready to take the company public, I tuned out.

"The wind has been blowing out of the east the past few days, right?" I whispered to Josie.

"Suzy, I'm trying to eat," she whispered back through a mouthful of chicken. "Whatever it is that has got your motor running will just have to wait. And in case you've forgotten, nobody has gotten killed."

"No, not yet," I said, making eye contact with her.

Josie studied my face then nodded.

"Okay, I'll play," she said, nodding at the outside deck.

I grabbed my phone from my pocket and held it up to my ear.

"This is Suzy," I said to the phantom caller. "Oh, hi. What? Hang on a sec." I removed the phone from my ear and looked at Josie. "We've got a problem at the Inn."

"Smooth," Josie whispered, shaking her head. Then she spoke loud enough to get everyone's attention. "What's going on?"

"Let's take it outside, so we don't interrupt dinner," I said, getting up out of my chair. I addressed the group. "I'm so sorry, but we need to take this call."

"Of course, duty calls, right?" Julian said, looking up at us before resuming his conversation with the two designers.

We walked out onto the porch, and I glanced back inside to make sure we weren't being watched then put my phone away. Josie gnawed on a chicken leg she'd brought with her from the table.

"Okay, Snoopmeister, you're on."

"Maria just told me a cover story about what happened with the Maltese that's a total lie."

"Maybe she's just embarrassed about the fact that her dog could have died out there," Josie said, tossing the leg bone in a nearby trash can.

"No, that's not it," I said, shaking my head. "She's not embarrassed. But she was definitely worried about what could have happened to Mellow. It's weird, but I think she's scared."

"What on earth does she have to be afraid of?" Josie said. "From what I've seen, her life looks pretty amazing."

"I have no idea."

"Well, thanks for clearing that up," she said, exhaling audibly. "Suzy, it's hard enough when we're dealing with actual problems. Why do you feel the need to make them up?"

"I'm not making anything up. I can't explain it, but that woman is afraid of something."

"Okay," Josie said. "I think we're done here. Can I go finish my dinner now?"

We both glanced out at the water when we heard a boat approaching. It pulled into the dock, and two men climbed out and looked up at the house. In the still night air, their voices were easily heard.

"Are you sure this is the right place?" one of the men said to the other.

34

"I think so. But I've never been here before."

"Julian said he would meet us at the dock."

I headed for the door and stuck my head inside.

"Julian, I think there are a couple guys down at the dock who are looking for you," I said.

Julian glanced at his watch, then got to his feet.

"They're early," he said, then wiped his mouth and tossed his napkin on the table. "I'll be right back."

Rock, one of the board designers, also started to get to his feet.

"No, finish your dinner, Rock," Julian said, waving him back into his chair. "I've got this. I'll be right back."

"Who is it, Julian?" Maria said, refilling her wine glass.

"It's Charlie and Gordo," he said, pausing in the doorway. "Those two are unbelievable." He glanced at me. "Between them, they win just about every event we sponsor, but they're never satisfied. Rock and Kirk just finished a new design, and, of course, they have to have the latest and greatest for tomorrow's race."

"They're in the storage shed," Rock said.

"Got it. Thanks."

Julian crossed the deck then quickly made his way down the stairs. He reached the dock, exchanged elaborate handshakes with both men, then they headed toward a large storage shed that sat near shore. Moments later, both men headed down the dock each carrying a large paddleboard and slid them into their boat. They waved, backed the boat away from the dock, then roared away. Julian came back up the stairs laughing.

"Those two are something else," he said.

"Why didn't they just wait to get the new boards in the morning?" I said. "Ow." I glanced back at Josie who had just punched me in the shoulder.

"Don't start," she whispered.

"They're going to try them out tonight," Julian said, shaking his head in amazement. "Can you believe that?"

"I suppose I could try," I whispered.

"What?"

"Nothing. It's a little dark to be out paddleboarding, isn't it?" I said.

"They say there's enough moonlight to see what they're doing," Julian said, still laughing.

"Why on earth would they do that? Ow."

"Are you okay?" Julian said, staring at me.

"Yeah, I'm fine. It's just my back," I said, glaring at Josie.

"Both of them are just incredibly dedicated," Julian said.

The rest of the group trailed outside and sat down. Full of food and drink, they sat quietly and stared out at the water.

"Dedication is one thing, but I can't imagine doing that, much less on the River at night," I said.

"Well, I can't argue with that. And you sure wouldn't catch me out there in the middle of the night. But it's how they make their living."

"Really? They can make a living doing that?"

"As long as they win enough races," Julian said, shrugging. "And since they do win a lot, they've been able to get some endorsements. In fact, they have one with us. And I think they just signed with Wet Water Fashions. Isn't that right, Emma?"

Emma nodded.

"Yeah, we just closed the deal with them. Personally, I think we paid those two idiots way too much, but it wasn't my call."

"Idiots?" I said, glancing over at Emma.

"They're out paddleboarding at night," she said, shrugging. "What would you call them?"

"Good point."

Chapter 4

I took a sip of my coffee then laughed again when I saw Captain and Chloe enjoying the breeze as the boat sped across the calm water. They had their front paws up on the bow, and their tails were like two synchronized metronomes. I nudged Josie who was sitting next to me, and she glanced at the dogs then shook her head.

"What a pair," she said, then stifled a yawn as she glanced toward the stern.

Chef Claire, tight-lipped and tense, was sitting quietly with Al and Dente who were sprawled out with their heads in her lap. On the deck in front of her were her paddleboard and kayak.

"She really doesn't want to do this," Josie said.

"I know, but she's too stubborn to back out," I said.

"A personality trait you, of course, are quite familiar with."

"Shut it," I said, taking another sip of coffee. "This is the third day in a row we've been over here. When was the last time that happened?"

"It's been a while," Josie said, glancing out over the water. "What a beautiful morning."

It was. The sun had reached the horizon, and a cloudless sky was beginning to take shape. Unlike our trip the other day when we'd found the Maltese, the Lake of the Isles was busy with boats. The event organizers had set up buoys to indicate the three courses for the individual events but had left a large section in the middle of the lake open for boats to come and go. Dozens of other boats filled with spectators ringed the outer edges, and I noticed many others watching from shore.

I slowed down as I entered the course area then spotted my mother's pontoon boat near the house where we'd had dinner last night. I pointed the boat in her direction and waved, but she was focused on whatever she was doing and didn't see us. Chef Claire gently slid out from underneath both Goldens then joined us.

"She must have left early this morning," Josie said. "What is she doing?"

"I think they're using her party boat as the registration area," I said, glancing around. "I thought she was nuts when she decided to organize this, but it's a pretty cool idea."

"As long as you don't have to do it," Josie said, grinning at Chef Claire. "Are you getting excited?"

"Yeah, I'm thrilled," Chef Claire deadpanned.

"Last chance to come to your senses," Josie said.

"No, I'm gonna do it."

"How does this work?" I said, glancing out at the course layouts.

"That's the swim course," Chef Claire said, pointing to the right. "A half-mile straight out, then back. Right next to it is the paddleboard area. When I finish my swim, you'll need to make sure my board is ready for me to get going."

"You mean right after you take a short break to throw up," Josie said.

"No, my plan is to throw up after I finish the paddleboard," Chef Claire said, managing a small laugh. "It looks like they've got a zig-zag course set up for the four miles. That headwind is definitely going to be a problem. And when I finish the paddleboard, I'll need my kayak over there."

She pointed toward the far right at two buoys that were gently bobbing in the wind.

"After that, all you need to do is wait until I finish the seven miles back to Clay Bay and take me straight to the emergency room," Chef Claire said, shaking her head.

"Do you have some sort of goal in mind?" Josie said. "You know, apart from surviving."

"I'm trying to finish in less than four hours."

"That sounds like a pretty good time," Josie said, shrugging. "I suppose it will only seem like a week."

"Four hours?" I said, frowning. "I couldn't do that in four hours with a gun to my head."

"How about if somebody was dangling a bag of doughnuts in front of you?" Josie said, laughing.

"Funny," I said, making a face at her. Then I turned to Chef Claire. "Well, it was nice knowing you."

"Yeah, we're gonna miss you," Josie said.

"You guys really need to work on your coaching skills."

My mother finally looked up from what she was doing and spotted us. She waved then gestured for us to come around to the side of her boat that was facing shore. I slowly maneuvered the boat through an area crowded with other craft, then Josie tossed a line to my mother who looped it around a railing. We climbed out and stepped onto her boat.

The dogs started to follow us, but Josie stopped all four with a firm command. Captain woofed his displeasure at her.

"Don't you grumble at me, Goofball," she said, rubbing the Newfie's head. "Just cool your jets."

Captain gave her another soft woof, then sat down on the deck and stared up at my mother.

"Somebody's not happy," she said, laughing as she gave me a hug. "Hello, darling."

"Good morning, Mom. What time did you get here?"

"A little after six," she said. "It was still dark. But I had a lot to do. There are coffee and muffins." She beamed at Chef Claire. "Are you ready for this?"

"Not really," Chef Claire said, shaking her head.

"Rule number one, dear," my mother said. "Never make promises or big decisions after you've had more than one glass of wine."

"Yeah, thanks, Mrs. C. I'll try to remember that."

"Well, better late than never, right? The registration area is right over there."

Chef Claire headed off, and my mother looked at me.

"How was your dinner last night?" she said.

"Dinner was fine," I said. "But your taste in men continues to come up a bit short, Mom."

"What was wrong with Matisse?" she said, raising an eyebrow at me.

"You mean, other than the fact the first thing out of his mouth was a comment about how he'd like to get me on my back?"

"He said that to you?" she said, frowning.

"Well, he said it in French hoping to get away with it," I said.

"What a pig," she said. "But he was so nice when I had dinner with him." She put her hands on her hips and stared out at the water before refocusing on me. "I'm sorry, darling." She patted my hand. "But don't worry, I'll keep looking."

Josie snorted, and my mother headed off toward the registration area. Chef Claire returned wearing a label with a number on it stuck to the front of her swimsuit. The number was also written in magic marker on her right arm.

"Okay, let's get this thing over with," Chef Claire said, climbing back into our boat.

"That's the spirit," Josie said, laughing.

I worked the boat away from my mother's and headed toward the swim course where dozens of participants were either standing in shallow water or waiting on boats for the event to begin. Then we heard a booming voice over the public-address system that had been set up on my mother's boat. Julian, the CEO of Paddles, welcomed everyone, spent a few minutes outlining how the 147 was going to work, then announced that there would be a post-event party at C's that evening. That bit of news caught Josie and me by surprise.

"My mother, right?" I said to Chef Claire.

"Yeah, she dropped it on me the other night," she said. "I forgot to mention it. It's no biggie. I've got the staff doing a bunch of appetizers and a couple of soups and stews. But that guy Julian is picking up the bar tab and capped it at ten grand. There was no way I was going to refuse an offer like that."

"Absolutely not," Josie said, stunned. "Ten thousand bucks. They must be selling a lot of boards."

"Wow," I said, glancing over at the Paddles CEO who was wrapping up his opening remarks. "That was incredibly generous of him. Either that or my mother applied some serious pressure."

"No, apparently he does it at all of their sponsored events," Chef Claire said. "The restaurant is going to be a zoo."

"All the more reason for you to take the night off," I said.

"Oh, don't worry, I'm only going to need the one," Chef Claire said, climbing out of the boat and sliding into the water.

Chapter 5

From the comfort of our boat, we watched over two hundred people of all ages become unrecognizable as they stroked and splashed their way through the water. What began as a tight grouping of bobbing heads and arms and legs soon spread out into a long line of swimmers as the leaders began to set a pace I had a hard time believing was possible. Chef Claire, identifiable through the binoculars only by the bright green swim cap she was wearing, was somewhere in the middle of the pack and like many of the other participants was doing her best not to get kicked in the face or slapped by nearby swimmers.

When the two leaders made the turn and began heading back toward us, I glanced at my watch then nudged Josie who was peering through her binoculars.

"Eleven minutes?" I said. "That can't be right, can it?"

She lowered the binoculars and glanced at her wrist. "No, that's what my watch says, too. Pretty amazing."

"How is that even possible?" I said, shaking my head.

"It's called the magic of exercise," she said, raising the binoculars.

"Magic, huh? I think I'll stick with card tricks."

45

The two leaders, now swimming with the wind, were even faster on the way back and they finished neck and neck in just under twenty minutes. They took several deep breaths then hopped on their paddleboards and began churning through the water before any of the other swimmers had come close to finishing.

"Those two must be the guys who showed up last night to pick up their new boards," I said, focusing on them through the binoculars.

"It looks like their practice session went well," Josie said. "They're motoring."

Chef Claire finished the swim in just over forty minutes, and she staggered briefly as she stood up in the knee-high water. Josie and I slid her paddleboard into the water and stared down at her. She removed her goggles and held the board with one arm as she struggled to catch her breath.

"How are you doing?" I said.

"Just peachy," she snapped.

"Hey, don't snark at me. It's not my fault."

Chef Claire climbed up on the paddleboard, took a few moments to find her balance, then Josie handed her the paddle.

"What was my swim time?" Chef Claire said, digging the paddle into the water.

"About forty minutes," Josie said.

"Should I even ask what the leaders did?" she said, glancing back over her shoulder as the board began to move through the water.

"Probably not," Josie said.

I slowly backed the boat toward shore, we sat down with the dogs and did everything in our power to keep them out of the water. They weren't sure who all the interlopers were that had invaded their favorite swimming spot, and they weren't very happy about it. But a snack followed by a nap took their minds off it, and Josie and I nibbled on the nosh plate we'd brought along.

"Hey, there you are," Maria said, idling the small boat she was piloting next to us. She had the Maltese tucked under one arm. Also on the boat were Layla and Kim, the two sales reps we'd met last night. All four dogs woke up and headed for the side of the boat to greet our visitors.

"Hi, folks," I said.

"Good morning," Maria said. "Look at these guys. Australian Shepherd, right?"

"Yeah, that's Chloe," I said. "She's my owner."

"She's gorgeous," Layla said. "They're all gorgeous. Who's the Newfie?"

"That's Captain," Josie said. "And those two are Al and Dente, Chef Claire's Goldens."

"Al Dente," Layla said, grinning. "That's funny."

"What do you think so far?" Maria said, nodding out at the water.

"That I'm glad I'm not out there," I said. "Are the two guys in the lead the same two who stopped by last night to pick up their new boards?"

"That's them," Maria said. "Pretty impressive, huh?"

"They were barely breathing hard when they finished the swim," I said.

"It's what they do," Maria said with a shrug.

"Where's the rest of your gang?" Josie said.

"They're up at the house doing some work," Maria said, suddenly unable to make eye contact. "They'll be down in a bit. After the race is over, a bunch of us are going to take the boards out if you want to join us."

I glanced at Josie then back at Maria.

"No, we'd love to, but we need to head over to the restaurant to give Chef Claire a hand getting ready for the party tonight."

"Smooth," Josie whispered.

"Thanks."

"Okay, then I guess we'll just see you later tonight," Maria said, pushing her boat away from ours. "Have fun."

We watched her slowly work the boat through the traffic as she headed toward the start of the kayak course.

"She's a terrible liar," I said.

"What on earth does she have to lie about?" Josie said.

"I have no idea," I said, raising my binoculars to check on Chef Claire's progress. "But she's really not very good at it."

"How's our girl doing?"

"She's struggling. That headwind is making it really tough sledding," I said. "We need to do something nice for her."

"Like a spa day?"

"We better make it a week."

Josie laughed and raised her binoculars.

"I can't believe it," she said.

"What is it?"

"Those two guys are already making the turn and heading back."

"How is that even possible?" I said, focusing my binoculars on the two men who continued to be in a dead heat.

49

"Well, for one, they're in amazing shape," Josie said. "And their technique and top of the line equipment have to make a huge difference."

"That and probably a whole bunch of steroids," I said, shaking my head. "Man, they're flying now that they're heading downwind. They're going to be done in about fifteen minutes."

"There's still a bunch of folks that haven't even finished their swim yet."

I lowered my binoculars then caught a glimpse of my mother trying to get our attention. She waved at us to come over, and I started the engine and slowly worked my way toward her party boat that was anchored about two hundred feet away.

"What's up, Mom?" I said, glancing up at her.

"Did you happen to bring sunscreen?"

"I did," I said, reaching into my bag and tossing it to her.

"Thanks, darling," she said, rubbing lotion on her arms and face. "I can't believe I forgot to bring it. Are you having a good time?"

"Yeah, it's pretty good," I said, nodding. "Have you been watching the two leaders?"

"I have," she said, glancing out at the two paddleboarders who continued to churn their way back toward shore. "Most impressive."

"They certainly are," Josie said.

"And they're pretty good on the water, too," my mother said with a grin.

"Mom!"

Josie snorted.

"I'm just looking, darling. What's wrong with that?"

"You could add their ages together and it still wouldn't…" I caught myself just in time and fell silent.

"Yes, darling?" my mother said, raising an eyebrow. "You have something to say?"

"No, I don't."

"I was just making an observation. It's nothing to lose your lunch money over."

"Here they come," Josie said, watching as both men crossed the paddleboard finish line.

They pushed their boards toward Maria's boat and headed for their kayaks that were already sitting in the water. They took about a minute to catch their breath and down a bottle of what looked like an energy drink, then climbed into their kayaks and headed back out to begin their seven-mile journey back to Clay Bay.

"It's definitely a two-man race," my mother said, staring out at the water and shielding her eyes to block the sun that was reflecting off the water. "There's nobody even close to them."

Josie and I both focused our binoculars on them and watched as they churned through the water using powerful, yet efficient, strokes. About a minute later, I saw something through the binoculars and flinched. I refocused then frowned and lowered the glasses and looked at Josie. She was already staring at me with a stunned expression.

"Did you just see that?" she said.

"I'm not sure," I said, grimacing. "What did you see?"

"It looked like the guy in the lead kayak just got shot."

"What?" my mother whispered.

"Yeah, that's what I saw, too," I said, peering through the binoculars.

The lead kayak had come to a sudden stop and was now drifting to the outer edge of the course as the wind shifted. The other participant, obviously unaware that anything had happened, continued paddling furiously, hunkered down to minimize the wind and focused intensely on the task at hand.

"Nobody else has noticed him," I said, sweeping the horizon with my glasses. "We need to get out there."

"Be careful, darling," my mother said.

"We will, Mom," I said. "But we need to leave the dogs here with you."

"Of course," my mother said.

"Okay, guys, follow me," Josie said, hopping onto my mother's boat trailed by all four dogs.

Josie rubbed all their heads, then jumped back into our boat.

"No, you guys stay here," Josie said.

"Hang on, darling."

"What?" I said.

"When you get out there, just wait with the kayak until Chief Abrams gets there," my mother said. "And it's probably a good idea to keep the kayak on the other side of your boat out of sight. We don't need two hundred people panicking in the water, so ask the Chief and the medical folks, if it's at all possible, if they can keep things low-key until most of the participants have left the area."

"We'll see what we can do."

I gave her a quick wave then slowly worked the boat along the shoreline. We stopped just long enough to slide Chef Claire's kayak out of the boat and set it on shore next to several others. I tried calling Chief Abrams cellphone, but it went straight to voicemail. I left a quick message for him to call me. I put my phone away then continued along the shoreline until I reached the outer edge of the kayak course. Then I made a left turn and accelerated toward the drifting kayak. Josie looked back at the spectators and participants through her binoculars then lowered them and glanced over at me.

"I still don't think anybody has noticed it yet," she said.

"I can't believe he got shot," I said, shaking my head.

"Right in the back."

"It doesn't make any sense," I said, slowing down as we approached the kayak and saw the man face down and slumped forward.

"Maybe it was a stray bullet. Have any hunting seasons started yet?"

"Just squirrel, I think," I said, putting the boat in neutral. "And maybe Canadian geese."

"Why would anybody want to shoot a defenseless squirrel?" Josie said, frowning.

"Why would anybody want to shoot a defenseless kayaker?" I said, nodding at the lifeless corpse that was bleeding out in the kayak.

"Geez, what a mess," Josie said, leaning over the side of the boat. She placed a finger on the man's neck to check for a pulse then sat down and shook her head. "He's gone."

I retrieved my phone and called the Chief again who answered on the second ring.

"Hey, are you watching this?" he said. "It's great, huh?"

"Yeah, at least it was," I said. "Where are you?"

"I'm on the north shoreline just before the turnaround point of the paddleboard event. Chef Claire just went by. I don't think she's having a lot of fun."

"She could be doing a lot worse," I said, glancing down at the kayak.

"Okay, I've got him," Josie said, her binoculars focused on the Chief's boat. "Chief, look out at the kayak course about thirty degrees to your right."

"Yeah, I see your boat. What's the matter?"

"We have a problem," I said. "Can you get over here?"

"Talk to me, Suzy," he said with his best police voice.

"You'll see when you get here," I said. "But take your time. There's no need to rush."

"Okay," he said, confused.

"And you might want to give Freddie a call."

"Really?"

"Yeah, I'm afraid so."

Chapter 6

We tied the kayak to our boat and did everything we could to ignore the dead guy a few feet behind us and focus on the race that continued unabated. Dozens of people had now completed the paddleboard event and were passing by our boat in their kayaks. Most of them were focused on the water in front of them as they paddled past. Fatigue mixed with frustration appeared to be the most popular facial expression as the participants grimly battled the stiff breeze. Chief Abrams' boat soon came into view from the northeast, and he gave all the participants a wide berth as he approached. He put the police boat in neutral and drifted until he came to a stop next to us. Josie tied both boats together, and he stepped onto ours already in full-on cop mode. He glanced down at the kayak then stood up and rubbed his forehead.

"Okay, first things first," he said. "You're sure he's dead?"

"Yeah, no doubt about it," Josie said. "And he was dead by the time we got here."

"How long ago was that?"

56

"Let's see," Josie said. "We both saw him get shot, then we dropped the dogs off with Suzy's mom, then headed straight out here. It couldn't have been more than five minutes from the time he got shot until we got here." She glanced at me. "Does that sound about right?"

"Yeah," I said. "And from the position of the hole in his back and the amount of blood in the kayak, he must have been shot through the heart. Did you get hold of Freddie?"

"I did," the Chief said. "He's on his way. The guy was one of the two leading the race, right?"

"Actually, he'd put some space between him and the other guy by then," Josie said. "He was probably about four or five lengths ahead."

"Did you see both kayaks through the binoculars when the shot was fired?" the Chief said.

I frowned and waited for my neurons to fire. The memory of the bullet hitting the man dominated my thoughts, and I wasn't exactly sure what else I'd seen. I looked at Josie who also seemed to be having trouble remembering.

"I think so," Josie said. "Right?"

"I'm not sure," I said, squinting hard to jog my memory bank. "You think the guy in the second kayak might have done it?"

"I'm not thinking anything yet," the Chief said. "I'm just asking."

We glanced out at the water when we heard a boat approaching. Freddie, our local medical examiner, slowed down, tied his boat to Chief Abrams' then made his way onto the police boat then climbed aboard ours.

"We really need to stop meeting like this," he said with a big grin.

"Not today, Freddie," I said.

"Somebody's grumpy," he said. "So, what's the deal with the guy in the kayak?"

Josie and I gave him the short version, and he listened closely. Then he stared down into the water for several moments.

"How the heck do I get down there to take a close look at him?"

"I was wondering the same thing," the Chief said. "I suppose we could borrow a kayak or a paddleboard."

"That's going to start attracting a lot of attention, Chief," I said.

"Yeah, you're right. I'd rather wait until the place cleared out a bit before we go much further," he said. "It looks like you're going to have to go for a little swim, Freddie."

"The things I do for this job," he said, shaking his head as he removed his shirt and running shoes. "When I get in, hand me my bag." He climbed over the side of our boat and lowered himself into the water. He pulled the kayak closer, then grabbed his bag from the Chief and set it on top of the kayak. He held onto the kayak with one hand and checked the victim for signs of a pulse.

"Okay, this guy has definitely sailed off into the sunset," Freddie said, removing his hand from the man's neck.

"Really, Freddie?" I said.

"What would you prefer?" he said, glancing up at me. "Kicked the bucket? Pushing up daisies? Bought the farm?"

"How about just saying he's dead?" I said, my voice rising a notch.

"I'm trying to mix it up a bit. I don't like repeating myself," Freddie said. "With you around, I need a whole inventory of death metaphors."

"With me around? What's that supposed to mean? I didn't shoot the guy."

"No, but you're always right in the middle of it every time something like this happens. I accepted the job up here because I thought I'd finally be able to get a little peace and quiet, but it's turning into Murder Central."

"Then move," I snapped.

"Okay, guys," Josie said softly. "Dial it down."

I took a few deep breaths, then glanced down into the water.

"Sorry, Freddie."

"Yeah, me too," he said, nodding.

"What the heck are you guys doing?"

The three of us on the boat turned around and saw Chef Claire, weather-beaten, exhausted, and very grumpy bringing her kayak to a stop next to us.

"Hey," I said. "How's it going?"

"Don't ask," she said. "I thought you were going to meet me after the paddleboard event."

"Yeah, well, something came up," I said.

"Like what?" she said, frowning.

"Dead guy in a kayak," Josie said.

"Are you kidding me? Not another one," Chef Claire said, still trying to catch her breath.

"That's what I said," Freddie called out.

"Freddie?"

"Yeah. How you doing, Chef Claire?"

"I've had better days. Where the heck are you?"

"In the water on the other side of the boat."

"Okay, I guess we might as well make this day even weirder," she said, shaking her head. "Let me guess. Based on personal experience, I'm gonna say the guy had a heart attack."

"No, he got shot," I said, tossing her a bottle of water she gulped down.

"Who was it?" she said.

"One of the two guys who was leading the race," Josie said.

"Why would anybody want to shoot him?" Chef Claire said. "They both seemed like good guys."

"You met them?" the Chief said.

"Just briefly before we started the swim," she said. "They actually wanted to have a drink with me later on after the race. I guess we'll need to cancel it now."

"Well, at least one of them will," Josie deadpanned.

Chef Claire smacked her paddle against the surface and sent a torrent of water onto the boat that drenched all three of us.

"Hey," Josie said.

"Way to go, big mouth," I said, glaring at Josie.

"Show some respect for the dead," Chef Claire said. "Okay, I need to get going. I'm not going to get caught in any crossfire, am I?"

"I doubt it," I said. "But this is the perfect excuse to withdraw from the race."

"No, I need to finish," she said, shaking her head. "I'll meet you at the main dock."

"Write if you get work," Josie called after her. Then she saw the hand gesture Chef Claire was giving her. "The mouth on that girl."

I wiped my face with a towel then tossed it to Chief Abrams. I leaned over the side of the boat to watch Freddie who had pulled the man's tee shirt up to examine the wound.

"Can you tell what kind of gun was used?" I said.

"My guess is a nine-millimeter," he said, lowering the tee shirt. "But I won't be able to confirm that until I get a better look at him. Give me a hand up."

Freddie handed his bag to the Chief, and we pulled him out of the water and back onto the boat. I handed him a fresh towel.

"Do they make nine-millimeter rifles?" I said to Chief Abrams.

"Sure, lots of them. You think somebody used a rifle instead of a handgun?"

"Well, if it was a handgun, the only person who could have shot him was the guy in the kayak behind him."

"That makes sense," he said. "And if it was him, that gun is already somewhere on the bottom of the River."

62

"I just can't remember if I could see both kayaks through the binoculars." I glanced over at Josie. "Can you?"

"No, the only image I've got is the sight of the bullet hitting him in the back."

"Freddie, what's your take on the impact angle?" I said.

"It looks like it was pretty much a straight on shot," he said.

"So, if the guy in the other kayak shot him, he would have had to have been directly behind him," I said.

"Yeah, that's the logical assumption," he said, nodding.

"But if it were a rifle, he would have been off to the side of the other kayak," I said. "You know, to give the shooter room to take the shot.

"Definitely," Freddie said. "Okay, I'm going to head home to change my clothes then head to the office. Just bring him by when you're ready, Chief."

"Will do."

"I'll see you guys later on at the restaurant," Freddie said, climbing back onto his boat.

"Oh, you're coming to the party? Good," I said.

"Chef Claire's food and an open bar?" he said, laughing. "Of course, I'm coming. I'm not a total idiot."

We waved goodbye as he drove off, then I looked back at the shoreline where the last of the kayakers were making their way into the water. Then I scanned the large stand of pines that grew near the edge of the water. The Chief followed my eyes and nodded.

"Yeah, those pines would definitely work," he said without having to be asked.

"How far do you think it is to those trees?"

"I'm gonna guess about three hundred yards."

"It wouldn't be that hard of a shot, right?"

"No. For someone who knows what they're doing with a good scope and a place to rest the gun, it's very doable. And with all the race noise, one gunshot probably wouldn't even get people's attention. Take the shot, then climb down and hop into your car or boat."

"Or maybe just head back to the house," I said, nodding at the massive A-frame.

Chapter 7

C's was jam-packed by the time we got there. The restaurant wasn't officially open for dinner, but the endless trays of appetizers streaming out of the kitchen told a different story. Josie and I had staked out our positions between a tray of stuffed mushrooms and another of bacon-wrapped barbeque shrimp.

"These shrimp are fabulous," Josie said.

"I can't believe I'm eating shrimp," I said, reaching for another.

"Bacon is a miracle worker," Josie said. "I can't believe Chef Claire actually showed up for work."

"What was her time?"

"Four hours and seven minutes."

"No wonder she's having trouble walking," I said.

"It's going to be worse tomorrow."

I caught a glimpse of Chief Abrams and my mother standing near the edge of the dining room. I waved them over, popped one more shrimp, then wiped my hands on a napkin.

"How are you doing, Mom?" I managed to mumble, then removed the shrimp tail that was hanging out of the corner of my mouth.

She put her hands on her hips and shook her head sadly at my manners, or lack thereof, then came in for a hug.

"You look tired," I said, reaching for a mushroom.

"I've been up since four," she said, glancing around the dining room and waving to several people. "But it was worth it. The race was a major success."

"Apart from the dead guy in the kayak, right?" Josie said through a mouthful of bacon.

"Yes, dear, apart from that," my mother said, grimacing.

"You got an update?" I said to the Chief.

"Freddie confirmed it was a nine-millimeter," he said. "The bullet was lodged in his chest. But we were right. He caught it in the heart, and Freddie said it must have exploded on impact. He was probably dead before his head hit the kayak."

"Did you interview the other guy? The one who won the race?"

"We did. Detective Williams and I spoke with him at length this afternoon."

Detective Williams worked for the state police, and we'd had our differences in the past. Most recently, we'd done battle when the three of us were trying to catch a killer, and I'd ended up getting shot in the shoulder by a flare gun. The detective and I had been able to put aside our differences, but from time to time, we still sparred and got snarky with each other.

"What did the guy have to say?" I said.

"He said he was so focused on the race, he didn't know anything had happened. He just thought he'd taken the lead because the other guy had gotten tired. And he said he never looked back once."

"Do you believe him?"

"Maybe," the Chief said, frowning. "It would have been really easy for him to do it. A couple of seconds to take the shot, then paddle off and toss the gun overboard later on during the race. He was all by himself during most of the race."

"What about the pine trees?" I said.

"We're going out tomorrow to mock the scene up and do some calculations," he said, then cut me off before I could speak. "And no, you can't come along."

"Why not?" I said, pouting.

"Because I said so."

Josie and my mother snorted.

"Gee, thanks, *Dad*," I said, glaring at him.

"Darling, the last time you tagged along on one of these adventures, you got shot."

"Ancient history, Mom."

"It's been four months," Josie said.

"Whose side are you on?" I said, glaring at her.

"Take a wild guess," Josie said, reaching for a mushroom.

"But what about all the people staying at the Anderson place?" I said to Chief Abrams.

"What about them?"

"Aren't you going to interview them?"

"Yes, we are," the Chief said. "Detective Williams and I have an appointment to speak with them tomorrow afternoon after we finish our work at the crime scene."

"You really think you're going to get anything out of them?"

"Why wouldn't we?" the Chief said, now annoyed.

"Because most people don't like opening up to cops," I said. "But I know them. I'm sure I'll be able to get a lot more out of them than you two will."

"No, I'm sure you won't," the Chief said, shaking his head.

"And why not?"

"Because you're not going," the Chief said, his voice rising enough to attract the attention of several bystanders.

I wheeled around to face my mother who gave me a blank stare.

"You put him up to this, didn't you?" I said to her.

"Maybe."

"I specifically asked you to stay out of my business, Mom."

"Asked?" she said, raising an eyebrow.

"Okay, maybe it was more of a command. But still, it's really none of your business."

"I'll concede the point, darling."

"Thank you," I said, then frowned at her. "You will?"

"Just as long as you're willing to concede that police work is none of yours."

Josie snorted again.

"Shut it." Then I stared at Chief Abrams. "C'mon, Chief. You know I can help."

"I'm sorry, Suzy," he said, shaking his head as he glanced at my mother. "But you're out of this one."

"This is so unfair."

"Yeah, go for wounded teenager," Josie deadpanned. "Good call."

I chewed my bottom lip and tossed my half-eaten mushroom aside.

"Suzy, the last time was a flare gun," the Chief said. "This time, somebody might end up firing a high-powered rifle at you."

"Why would anybody want to shoot me?" I said, glancing around at all three.

"Rhetorical, right?" Josie said to my mother who laughed way too loud.

I stormed off to the lounge and took a seat at the bar. A harried Millie worked her way around the two other bartenders who were struggling valiantly to keep up with the drink orders and came to a stop directly across the bar from me.

"What a zoo," she said. "Can I get you anything?"

"No, I'm just going to be here for a minute until I cool off," I said, glancing around the lounge.

"Problem?"

"Yeah, three of them," I said, noticing Josie who was approaching with a big grin. "And here comes one now."

"Hi, Josie," Millie said.

"Hey, Millie," Josie said, coming to a stop right next to me. "I'm looking for a petulant teenager with a fondness for

70

snooping and chocolate and was wondering if you've seen her."

I did a slow burn and stared straight ahead. Millie laughed and shook her head at us then headed off to the other end of the bar where customers were stacked three deep.

"Thanks for the support in there," I said, maintaining my stare.

"You're welcome. Always happy to help out."

"I expect that sort of crap from my mother," I said, still not making eye contact. "But you?"

"Suzy, when people start getting shot with rifles it's time to let the professionals handle things."

"And after everything I've done for Chief Abrams, this is how he treats me?"

"Stop being such a baby," she said. "Just stay out of it. In a few days, it'll all be over."

"In a few days, those people will be gone," I said, finally making eye contact.

"And you think one of them killed the guy in the kayak?" Josie said.

"I'm positive."

"And you know this how?"

"Let's call it a hunch."

"I guess that's a word for it," Josie said, shrugging. "I probably would have gone with something else from your *grasping at straws* collection, but whatever works for you."

"You're not helping."

"I'm not here to help," she said softly. "I'm here to see if you're ready to go home and play with the dogs."

"I am," I said, sliding off my stool. "Did Chief Abrams say what time he and Detective Williams were heading over to the crime scene tomorrow?"

"Stop it."

"What?"

"I said stop it," she said, her voice rising. "But for the record, I think they plan on being there all day. So, there's no way you'll be able to get the boat in without them seeing you."

"No, I'm sure you're right," I said, grinning at her. "I wouldn't."

"I can't believe you," she said, shaking her head.

"What?"

"You're not going to take the boat. You're going to drive over, aren't you?"

"Nothing gets past you."

Chapter 8

I crossed the first span of the Thousand Islands bridge that led from the mainland to Wellesley Island then exited the highway a few miles before reaching the later spans that led to Canada. It took me a few minutes to remember how to get to the Anderson place, but my memory bank eventually recalled the times when I had been either joyriding in the summer or snowmobiling in the winter. I parked in back with my car invisible to those on the River side of the house and strolled down a stone path that led to the deck. At the bottom of the steps, I glanced out at the River and spotted the Chief and Detective Williams chatting on the police boat that appeared to be anchored near the spot where the kayaker had been shot.

"Try to ban me, will you?" I whispered as I slowly trudged up the stairs and onto the deck.

I heard voices inside the house and gently tapped on the sliding glass doors. Moments later, Maria, cradling the Maltese under an arm, slid one of the doors open. She seemed startled but happy to see me.

"Suzy, what a nice surprise," Maria said.

"Hi," I said, grinning back and rubbing the dog's head. "How are you doing, Mellow?"

"She's great," Maria said. "What's up?"

"Well, I was just on my way across the border to do a little shopping, but I thought I'd stop by on my way to thank you again. Both the race and the party were major hits with everyone. Apart from, well, you know."

"Yes," she said, grimacing. "It was just horrible. I can't believe anybody could do something like that. Would you like to come in?"

"I guess I could stay for a few minutes," I said, stepping inside.

"We were just about to have lunch," Maria said. "Please, join us."

"That sounds great. Thanks."

The rest of the group was lounging in a sitting area near the table where we'd eaten dinner the other night. They glanced up when I approached and waved and welcomed me. The only vacant spot was on a couch next to Matisse, and I flinched when he smiled at me and patted the cushion inviting me to sit down. I tentatively sat down and inched my way to the furthest edge. Emma, the woman who worked for Wet Water Fashions, noticed my discomfort and laughed.

"Don't worry, Suzy," she said, glancing at Matisse. "The couch doesn't recline."

I flushed red with embarrassment when the group laughed. Except for Matisse who was annoyed by Emma's comment.

"Well, if anybody would know about reclining, it would be you, Emma," Matisse said, glaring at her.

An uncomfortable silence followed that was eventually broken by Maria who announced that lunch was served. We made our way to the table, and I found a seat between Emma and Rock, one of the board designers. Matisse sat down directly across from me and made eye contact.

"Je voudrais m'excuser pour mon comportement l'autre nuit," Matisse said.

"Uh-oh," Emma said, scowling. "There he goes again."

"No, it's okay," I said. "He was only apologizing for the other night." I looked across the table and nodded at him. "Vos excuses sont acceptées. Merci."

"Okay," Rock said, reaching for the salad bowl. "Apology offered and accepted. Let's eat."

"How long are you guys sticking around?" I said, spooning a serving of lasagna onto my plate.

"We had been planning on leaving this morning," Julian said, not looking up from his phone. "But then the situation with Charlie happened." He tossed his phone aside, then stared off into the distance and exhaled loudly. "Poor Charlie."

Either he was completely grief-stricken or a very good actor. Maria, sitting next to him, reached out and patted his hand. Julian rubbed his forehead then raised his glass.

"To Charlie. May he rest in peace."

"To Charlie," the rest of the group said as they also raised their glasses in tribute.

"So, you've decided to stay for a while?" I said, taking a bite of the lasagna. For the record, it was very good and fell just short of the coveted knee-buckler award.

"We'll probably leave tomorrow," Julian said. "At least Maria and I will. We need to get down to Mexico."

"You have another event down there?" I said, taking a bite of the roasted red peppers with mozzarella that had been marinated in olive oil, garlic, and red chili flakes. They got my undivided attention, and I took a second bite. "Wow. These are fantastic."

"Thanks," Maria said. "I learned how to make those when we were in Italy last year. What a trip that was, huh?"

"One of the best," Julian said, beaming at her. Then he focused on me. "No, there's no event. The factory where we make all our boards is in Mexico. It's in Punta Chicado."

"I'm not familiar with it," I said.

"It's this great little surf town just north of Matazlan," Julian said. "And I need to get down there and make sure our new production schedule is on track."

"I can be there in a couple of days," Rock said.

"That works," Julian said, nodding. "What about you, Kirk?"

"Yeah, that's fine," he said, his voice flat and distant.

"Somebody's grumpy," Layla said, laughing.

"I'm not grumpy," Kirk said. "I was just thinking about Charlie."

"Yeah," Layla whispered. "I'm sorry. That was insensitive of me."

"Forget it," Kirk snapped, then stabbed his lasagna with a fork. He chewed and stared off in silence.

"Hey, lighten up," Rock said to Kirk. "Charlie's gone, and there's nothing we can do about it."

While I couldn't argue with his logic, his comment still seemed harsh. I glanced around the table and noticed that everyone was suddenly preoccupied with their food.

"I wouldn't mind getting out of here today," Emma said. "I've got a ton of work waiting for me back in the office."

"Where is your office?" I said, going for casual.

"Well, our headquarters are in New York," she said. "But I work out of our L.A. office." Then she looked at Julian. "Maybe I can catch a late flight out of Ottawa tonight. How long do you think the cops are going to want to talk to us?"

I'd been trying to figure out a way to slip the Chief's visit into the conversation and almost blurted out a thank you to her before I caught myself.

"I have no idea," Julian said.

"The police are stopping by?" I said, sneaking a peek out at the water where the Chief and Detective Williams were still doing their thing.

"Yeah, they want to interview all of us," Maria said. "I guess that makes sense since we were the only people in the area who actually knew him."

"Don't bet on it," Rock said, snorting softly.

"Please, don't start, Rock," Julian said, shaking his head.

"You know the sort of people he ran with," Rock said.

My neurons flared, and my Snoopmeter turned itself on. I toyed with my food and listened closely.

"Yes, I certainly do," Julian said, then turned to me, apparently feeling the need to offer an explanation. "Charlie had a tendency to get himself into some trouble from time to time."

"I see," I said, nodding.

I didn't have a clue what he was referring to. But I maintained eye contact in an attempt to keep him talking.

"Charlie had a bit of a gambling problem," Julian said.

Emma laughed and looked around the table.

"A bit of a problem? That's like saying Matisse has a little thing for the ladies," she said.

"I was trying to be kind, Emma," Julian snapped. "How about showing a little respect for the dead?"

"Fine," Emma whispered. "It's just that I'd never say that someone who owed half a million in gambling debts might have a *bit of a problem.*"

"Point taken," Julian said, glaring at her. "Now, can we please change the subject?"

"Half a million?" I whispered, more to myself than the others.

"Yes," Julian said. "At least that's what he admitted to. It could have been more."

"What did he bet on?" I said.

"Anything and everything," Rock said. "Yesterday, he wanted to bet me five grand it was going to rain. I told him there's was no way I was going to bet with him on that."

79

"Because you thought it was stupid to bet on the weather?" I said, frowning at him.

"No, because he never paid up when he lost," Rock said, looking at me like I was a total idiot. "And that's the reason he was hunted down."

"We don't know that," Julian said.

"You got a better explanation?" Rock said, staring at the CEO.

"No, I don't," Julian said, toying with his salad.

"I'm so sorry, Suzy," Maria said. "This is a horrible topic to be discussing over lunch."

"No, it's fine. Don't worry about it," I said, waving it off. "I'm just sorry you lost such a good friend."

I glanced around to see if my *good friend* comment provoked any response but got nothing from the group.

"Where did Charlie live?" I said, helping myself to a second helping of the lasagna.

"Well, he was on the road pretty much year round," Julian said. "But I think he grew up somewhere in New York. Was it Syracuse?"

"Rochester," Rock said.

"That's right," Julian said. "If I remember, he kept an apartment there. You know, as sort of a home base. I doubt if he got there very often."

80

"I don't know how he could have," Rock said, shaking his head. "His schedule was crazier than ours."

I glanced around the table, mid-bite, and caught Matisse and Emma sharing a look that could only be described as one of angry lovers on the verge of reconciling. I found it interesting, but not very useful and filed it away.

"Have you seen the other kayaker?" I said. "I'm sorry, I don't remember his name."

"Gordo? No, we haven't," Julian said. "After the race, the police wanted to talk with him. And when they finished, I think he just went back to his hotel room."

"He was devastated," Maria said.

"They must have been very good friends," I said.

"They were inseparable," Julian said. "I talked to him on the phone this morning. He's still a complete mess and has decided to just hole up in his room until the cops give him the okay to leave town."

"Speaking of cops," Maria said, nodding at the glass doors that led out to the deck.

She headed toward the doors, and I wondered if I had time to make it to the bathroom before the Chief and Detective Williams entered. I was halfway out of my chair when Emma stopped me with a question.

81

"What's it like running a dog hotel?" she said. "It sounds like a pretty good way to spend the day."

"Yeah, at times like this, I miss not being there," I said, glancing at the two cops who were still standing near the door chatting with Maria.

"What?" Emma said, frowning.

"It's just a figure of speech," I said, settling back into my chair, caught red-handed.

Maria led Chief Abrams and Detective Williams to the table and handled introductions. When the Chief and the detective saw me, they both flinched but recovered quickly.

"And, of course, you both must know Suzy," Maria said.

"Yes, we certainly do," the Chief said, his face unreadable. "Hello, Suzy."

"Hi, Chief," I chirped, deciding to go for upbeat. "Hello, Detective Williams."

"Nice to see you, Suzy," the detective said, nodding.

"Oh, I seriously doubt that," I said softly as I took another bite of the roasted peppers.

"Before I forget," the Chief said. "Remind me later that I need to have a little chat with you."

"Will do, Chief," I said. "I was just in the neighborhood on my way to Ottawa and thought I'd pop in to say hi."

"Ottawa, huh?" the Chief said.

82

"Yes, I thought I'd do a little shopping. Can I pick anything up for you while I'm there?"

"A stack of restraining orders would be nice," he deadpanned. "I'm running low, and I have a feeling I'm going to need a bunch of them very soon."

"Sure, sure."

I pushed my plate away and stood up. I looked around the table and gave them my best smile.

"Thanks so much for lunch," I said. "I'll get out of here and let you folks talk. If I don't see you again before you go, safe travels. And I hope we get a chance to do the race again next year. Once again, I'm so sorry for your loss."

I gave Maria a hug, rubbed the Maltese's head, then waved to the rest of the group and made a beeline for the door. I got halfway down the stairs then heard footsteps behind me. I continued down the stairs until I reached the lawn then turned around. The Chief was standing on the bottom step, eyes narrowed and tight-lipped.

"Are you trying to get me fired, Suzy?"

"Fired? What on earth are you talking about?"

"Who do you think I'm talking about?" he said, giving me a cold stare.

"My mother threatened to fire you?" I said, stunned.

"Let's just say she's dropped some serious hints and leave it at that."

"There's no way I'd ever let that happen, Chief."

"Oh, *you* wouldn't let it happen. That makes me feel so much better," he said, shaking his head. "Why do you find it impossible to follow even the simplest of requests."

"Yeah, I really need to start working on that."

"Don't start, Suzy. I'm not in the mood. Do you want me to arrest you?"

"Oh, come on, Chief. Where's the fun in that?" I said, going for playful.

It didn't work, and his anger ratcheted up a notch.

"Don't push me on this one, Suzy. I've got half a mind to lock you up just to make my point."

"Arrest me for what? Eating lunch?"

"Oh, I don't know. I'm sure Detective Williams and I can come up with something. Like obstruction of a criminal investigation. Or impersonating a police officer."

"I thought that was your thing," I said with a big grin.

My reference to the time when I had first used the *impersonating a cop* reference to torment him and Detective Williams struck a nerve. They had gotten wedged in a bathroom door during our last adventure and allowed the killer to escape from the hospital briefly before being

84

captured. Then I'd gotten shot, and things rapidly went downhill after that. But I wasn't shy about dredging up the *stuck in the door* taunt whenever I needed to deflect or buy a little time.

Like right now.

"Suzy, you need to dial it down."

"I'm not doing anything," I said, pouting. "You're the one getting all snarky. And if you're worried about my mother, that's your problem. You need to grow a pair, Chief."

The Chief took several deep breathes to calm himself, then locked eyes with me.

"All I'm asking is for you to stay out of the way."

"No problem," I said, shrugging. "Didn't I leave as soon as you guys showed up?"

"Why do I even bother?" he said, starting to head back up the stairs.

"Aren't you even going to ask if I figured anything out?" I said, putting my hands on my hips.

"Sure," he said, turning back around. "Did you figure anything out?"

"I did."

"And?"

"And what?" I said, frowning at him.

85

"Aren't you going to tell me what it is?"

"Absolutely not. Figure it out yourself."

I stormed off and lumbered toward my car, then tore out of the driveway and hit the road for home. I headed straight for my mother's house where we proceeded to have the biggest fight we'd ever had. I finally arrived home, emotionally drained, my insides churning, my neurons scrambled and firing blanks. Josie and Chef Claire looked up when I walked into the living room and sunk into one of the couches.

"How did your fight with your mother go?" Josie said.

"How the heck did you know that?"

"She called a minute ago looking for you," Chef Claire said.

"I can't believe she still had more to say. I thought she'd run dry by the time I left," I said, gently rubbing Chloe's head who had jumped up on the couch to join me.

"She was crying," Josie said softly.

"I made my mother cry?" I said, crushed by the news.

"Yes," Chef Claire. "And she was also swearing like a sailor."

"Oh, yeah," Josie said, nodding. "There was lots of swearing. I don't think I've ever heard some of those combinations before."

86

"I'm gonna have to figure out a way to apologize," I said, exhausted from the past hour.

"Well, you better hurry up," Josie said. "She's meeting you for lunch tomorrow at noon at C's."

"Okay," I said, nodding. "At least it's a public place. She wouldn't dare to try anything there."

"She's got quite a mouth on her when she wants to use it," Chef Claire said, chuckling.

"What did she call me?"

"Oh, I'm not comfortable using that sort of language," Chef Claire said, shaking her head.

Chapter 9

After dinner, I left Josie and Chef Claire in the living room where they were playing with the dogs in front of the fire and headed outside to relax on the porch with Chloe. I needed some alone time to prepare for my apology lunch with my mother as well as figure out a way to either work my way back into the Chief's good graces or come up with a credible way to conduct my own investigation.

The temperature had dropped considerably since the sun had slipped below the horizon. The sunset, a beautiful mix of blues and orange, was long gone, and I couldn't miss the chill in the wind that was now blowing out of the north. I stretched out on a recliner and wrapped a thick blanket around me until I was cocooned from the cold. Chloe was snoozing comfortably but still trying to take full possession of my lap even as she slept, and I sipped from a snifter of B&B, a concoction my good friend Rooster had successfully introduced me to a few years ago despite my original protests. At first, drinking a combination of French brandy and Benedictine had sounded horrible. But when Rooster poured some into a snifter and microwaved the drink for about twenty seconds, I fought my way through the initial fumes that overwhelmed then cleared my sinuses and took a sip. From that point on, I was a big fan of the drink as well as the Benedictine monks that had the brilliant idea to combine the two. And while I wouldn't necessarily make a good follower of the Benedictine philosophy, most notably due to my personal shortcomings on the obedience front and my inability to adhere to long periods of silence, my respect for their dedication and commitment to their traditions is immense.

Not to mention how good the booze they make is.

I took a small sip and again marveled how the liquid seemed to be giving my insides a long, warm hug. I do have a basic understanding of how brandy is made, but the creation of Benedictine is a complete mystery to me other than I know that a couple dozen plants and spices are used to make it. But since, according to legend, less than a handful of people on the planet know the actual recipe, my ignorance doesn't bother me.

My neurons flared when I drifted onto the question of why I was so easily satisfied not knowing how the warm, magical liquid I enjoyed on a regular basis was made, while not knowing the identity of the person who had shot someone I'd never even met before was driving me crazy. And if Chief Abrams and Detective Williams didn't soon relent and change their position about letting me back under the tent when it came to the latest facts and evidence concerning the case, I worried that I'd be stuck in an endless loop as my neurons bounced inside my head with no destination or landing spot to coalesce around.

I savored another sip of my B&B then set the snifter down on the table next to me. Chloe's fur fluttered briefly as a gust of wind whipped across the porch. I stroked her back, and she stretched out all four legs in unison then licked my hand. I shivered as another gust raced past, and I knew that Mother Nature was having a little early fall fun with me. But I didn't let her reminder of winter's approach concern me. Hopefully, we still had around six weeks of sweater-weather as the fall foliage arrived, was enjoyed by all, then was blown away leaving many of the trees barren until spring. From that point, we were a hop and a skip away from Thanksgiving, then a mere four weeks from Christmas. And a few days after Santa had come and gone, we'd be on our way to Cayman.

I flinched when my neurons fired, then I broke into a grin.

Cayman.

I grabbed my phone, and Rocco answered on the third ring.

"Hey, Suzy," Rocco said, speaking loud to make himself heard above the noise of the restaurant. "Give me a sec to get someplace quieter." Moments later, he came back on the line. "How are you doing?"

"I'm good, Rocco. Everybody's good. And you?"

"Fantastic."

"Teresa and the kids?"

"Even better."

"Glad to hear that. Tell them I said hi. It sounds like you guys are busy tonight," I said, reaching for the snifter of B&B.

"Yeah, big night. A couple of cruise ships came in today, and I think my new marketing strategy is starting to pay off."

"Which one is that?" I said, frowning.

"The one where I agree to feed and water the ships' concierges if they have the correct answer to the question they get asked all the time."

"You mean the question; Can you recommend a good place to eat on Grand Cayman?" I said, laughing.

"Nothing gets past you," he said. "Did you call just to say hi, or do you need something?"

"Both."

"Okay, now that the preliminaries are out of the way, how can I help you?"

"You used to be a criminal, right?" I said.

"Those are just vicious and unfounded rumors," he said, laughing.

"Don't worry. Your secret is safe with me. We had a problem at the 147 the other day."

"Oh, that's right, the water triathlon. How did it go?"

"Great. Apart from the leader of the race getting shot in his kayak."

"Dead?"

"Very much so," I said.

"Well, don't look at me. I've been down here the whole time."

"Funny," I said. "The reason I'm calling is that the victim apparently lived in Rochester when he wasn't on the road. That was part of your old territory, right?"

"Among others, yes, it was. But I'm going to need a bit more, Suzy. I'm not making the connection."

"Apparently, the victim had a bit of gambling problem," I said.

"I see. Define a bit of a problem."

"The word is that he owed half a million. Maybe even more," I said, taking a sip of B&B.

"That's a big number," Rocco said.

"And enough for somebody to get killed over, right?"

Rocco laughed. I waited impatiently for him to finish.

"Suzy, an unpaid gambling debt of a half million bucks is enough to get you chopped up into little pieces and all the parts mailed to your family members."

I grimaced as the mental image of several oddly shaped packages sitting under a Christmas tree popped into my head. I chased it away with another sip and set the snifter on the table.

"Thanks for that visual, Rocco."

"Hey, you asked. So, what do you need from me?"

"I know you've been out of the business for a long time, but do you know who handles book in the Rochester area?"

"Handles book?" he said. "Have you been watching too many cop shows again?"

"No, but I did happen to catch Casino again the other night," I said, laughing. "But you know what I mean."

"I do," Rocco said. "There's only a couple of people down there big enough to handle an account like that. Or be willing to carry that much debt before taking action to get it back."

"So, you do know who it might be?"

"Yes, I have a pretty good idea who it is."

"That's great," I said, sitting up in the recliner and getting an annoyed snort out of the sleeping Chloe. "What's his name?"

"I can't tell you that, Suzy," Rocco said.

"Why not?"

"Suzy, I've spent way too many years putting distance between me and my previous life. And now you expect me to tell you the name of the guy who runs one of the biggest illegal bookmaking shops in New York state?"

"Why not?"

"You must be way off your game today. I'm going to pretend you didn't ask a question that dumb," Rocco said, his voice rising a notch.

"There's no need to get snarky, Rocco."

"You expect me to tell you the guy's name so you and the Chief can drive down there and start asking him a bunch of questions?"

"No, I'd be going by myself," I said, downing the last mouthful of my drink.

"Oh, that makes it so much better," he said. "You want to confront a crime boss about his operation all by yourself. And knowing you, probably insinuate that he might have been the guy who had the kayaker shot in the head."

"Back," I said.

"What?"

"He got shot in the back," I said softly.

"I don't care if he got shot in his pinky toe," Rocco said, barely able to contain his anger. "That is not a question you just casually toss out to a guy like Pizza Oven Paulie."

Rocco fell silent for several seconds. I was pretty sure he spent most of the time kicking himself for blurting the guy's name out.

"Pizza Oven Paulie?" I cooed.

"I can't believe I let that slip. Forget I said that. You need to forget that name immediately, Suzy."

"It's a little hard to forget a name like that, Rocco. Pizza Oven Paulie kind of rolls off the tongue, wouldn't you say?"

"Suzy, you're very lucky I'm not there at the moment," Rocco said.

"Relax, Rocco. All I want to do is ask the guy a few questions. And I won't be bringing the cops with me so he won't have to worry about that."

"The guy worries about everything. How do you think he manages to stay in business?"

"By making really good pizza?" I deadpanned.

"Trust me, that is not how he got his nickname," Rocco said. "You want to hear the story?"

"Uh, not at the moment," I said, frowning.

"Good call. You and Chief Abrams always partner up on this sort of thing. Why are you cutting him out of the loop?"

"Actually, he's the one doing the cutting," I said.

"Oh, I get it," Rocco said. "Your mother had a little chat with the Chief after you got shot, didn't she?"

"Yeah, him and several others."

"Listen to your mother, Suzy."

"Sure, sure," I said, nodding. "So, how do I find this Pizza Oven Paulie?"

"You don't."

"C'mon, Rocco," I said. "Consider it a favor to a friend."

"Don't you dare play the friendship card with me on this one," he snapped. "He's a dangerous man, Suzy."

"It's not like I'm going to walk in there and accuse him of killing the guy. I'll just buy him a beer and a slice and tell him I'm…"

"Tell him what?"

"I'm sure I'll think of something," I said, rubbing my forehead. "C'mon, Rocco. We're talking about a murder here."

"No!"

"Geez, Rocco. There's no need to yell at me."

96

"No," he whispered. "Is that better?"

"Funny," I snapped. "Okay, then I'll just have to track him down on my own."

I waited out another extended silence.

"Please, don't do this, Suzy," Rocco said. "But if you're going to insist on sticking your nose in, just give Paulie's name to the Chief and let him handle it."

"Absolutely not."

"Why not?"

"On principle, mostly," I said. "I'm determined to prove a point here."

"Determined, huh?"

"Yeah, what would you call it?"

"Stubborn. Obstinate. Recalcitrant. Take your pick."

"Tomato, tomahto."

"You're *determined* to talk to Paulie?"

"I am."

I waited out another long silence. I smiled to myself. I hated boxing Rocco in like this, but I was convinced I was onto something, and like the old saying goes, you can't make an omelet without breaking a few eggs. Before I had time to mentally recite some of the other ingredients in my favorite omelet, Rocco finally responded.

"Okay, I'll help you out," he said, slowly. "But I have some conditions."

"Shoot."

"Oh, let's hope it doesn't come to that."

"Funny."

"I wish I was joking," Rocco said softly. "First, do not under any circumstances call him Pizza Oven Paulie. It's either sir or Mr. Provincial, got it?"

"Got it. But why is he called Pizza Oven Paulie?"

"You really want to know?"

"Not really. But I should probably know a bit more about who I'm dealing with," I said, shrugging.

"Okay. Maybe knowing how he got his nickname will knock some sense into you. It's one of his favorite techniques to teach people a lesson. You know, behavior modification 101. Whenever a gambler would get way behind on his account, Paulie's first move was to shove one of the guy's hands into an eight-hundred-degree oven."

"Yuk."

"Yeah, I know. Pretty brutal, huh?"

"No, I was just wondering what that does to the taste of the pizza."

"Unbelievable," Rocco said, exhaling into the phone. "By the way, did the guy who got shot have any burn marks or scars on his hands?"

"I have no idea," I said, making a mental note to check with Freddie.

"It might be worth checking out. Second, the guy's a major dog lover."

"Really? Then he can't be all bad," I said, shrugging.

"No, I've always liked Paulie," Rocco said. "He loves big dogs, especially Labrador retrievers."

"Dogs, as in plural?"

"Yeah, I've seen him with up to four or five at a time. That could come in handy for you."

"Thanks, Rocco."

"And he's a major flirt, so be prepared for that," he said. "He loves women with a sense of style."

"I can handle that."

"So, don't wear flannel or your work boots," he said, laughing.

I waited it out, fuming.

"Anything else?" I said, tight-lipped.

"Wear your hair down with just a touch of makeup. And he's a big fan of red lipstick. If you're up for it."

"Is this guy a gangster or a fashion critic?"

99

"Paulie can be a critic about everything, so don't push his buttons," Rocco said, turning serious. "You'll need to give me a day or two."

"For what?"

"To give me enough time to call and prepare him for the pain in the butt that's about to descend on him."

"You're going to call him? You'd do that for me?"

"Of course, I'm going to call him. Do you think I'd let you walk in there unannounced?"

"Aren't you sweet."

"Thanks. But don't spread it around. You'll ruin my reputation," he said. "Paulie does owe me a couple of favors."

"Favors for what?"

"You don't want to know," Rocco said. "But this is more about self-preservation, Suzy."

"You think Paulie might come after you if I screw things up?"

"I'm talking about your mother, Suzy. If she finds out I introduced you to Pizza Oven Paulie, I'm a dead man."

"I won't tell a soul."

"Hang on a sec," he said. "I just remembered. She and Paulie are pretty tight. At least, they used to be. You showing

100

up might not be that big of a deal as long as you behave yourself."

"My mother is tight with this guy?"

"Let's say they go way back and leave it at that," Rocco said. "But just to be safe, don't bring your mother up unless he mentions her."

"Okay," I said, now thoroughly confused. "So, you'll call me?"

"I will," Rocco said. "And don't do anything until you hear back from me."

"Got it," I said, my neurons still trying to make sense of the last bit of news. "My mother is tight with a gangster?"

"I think they had a little thing going on several years ago. But you didn't hear that from me."

"Really? A thing?"

"Yeah. Fortunately for both of us, they parted on good terms."

Chapter 10

I arrived at C's at noon sharp, parked in back of the restaurant, and entered through the kitchen. Chef Claire glanced up at me and nodded a hello.

"I'd give you a hug, but my hands are full at the moment," she said.

"So, I see," I said, staring at the pans stuffed with prime rib roasts. "Is my mother here yet?"

"I think she just walked in," Chef Claire said, efficiently sliding all four pans into the oven. "Good luck."

I waved over my shoulder then headed through one of the swinging doors that led into the dining room. My mother was sitting at her private table in a far corner of the restaurant and spotted me immediately. I got a small nod but no wave and swallowed hard as I approached the table.

"Hi, Mom," I said, sitting down across from her.

"Hello, darling," she said, setting her menu aside before folding her hands in front of her and fixing her stare on me.

It was one of her better ones.

"I want to apologize for my behavior yesterday, Mom."

"Uh-huh," she said, picking her menu back up and casually perusing it.

"No, I'm serious," I said. "I shouldn't have said some of the things I did."

"Name one," she said, flipping to a new page.

Okay, I said to myself, she wants specificity. This could end up being a long afternoon. I chewed my bottom lip and took a few deep breaths.

"Well, I probably shouldn't have called you an intrusive busybody."

"Uh-huh," she said, turning to another page in the menu.

"And that crack about how you're a real mother of a smothering hoverer was completely uncalled for."

"I see."

"Although I did like the alliteration of that one," I deadpanned.

Her frown cracked with a hint of a smile then it disappeared.

"Is there anything else you'd like to say?"

"Just that I'm really sorry, Mom. And I feel horrible about making you cry," I said, reaching across the table to grab her hand.

"Made me cry?" she said, frowning. "Where on earth did you hear that nonsense? But I have been dealing with allergies lately."

"Okay, Mom. Whatever you say," I said, shaking my head. "Do you forgive me?"

"Yes, darling, I do," she said, squeezing my hand before removing hers. She sat back in her chair. "I'm going to have the chicken Caesar. What do you feel like?"

"That sounds good," I said, pushing my menu to one side.

"We'll order just as soon as the Chief and Detective Williams get here," she said, giving me a small smile.

"They're coming? Why did you invite them?" I said, surprised by the news.

"So we can get an update on the investigation, of course," she said. "Just because you aren't directly involved doesn't mean we can't follow along."

My neurons flared. I tried to make sense of why she was suddenly willing to let me participate in a conversation about the investigation when yesterday she'd basically threatened to disown me if I got anywhere near it. Then a lightbulb switched on, and I shook my head in disbelief.

"The Chief called you, didn't he?"

"Yes, as a matter of fact, I did speak with the Chief last night," she said, fiddling with her napkin.

"And he told you that he and Detective Williams didn't get anything useful out of the people staying at the Anderson place, right?" I said, going for mildly surprised but probably coming across as smug.

"Maybe."

"So, now the three of you want to know what I learned?"

My mother gave me a blank stare, then shrugged.

"We're all under a lot of pressure, darling," she whispered.

"We?"

"The town," she said, leaning forward with her elbows on the table. "Do you know how many killings Clay Bay has had over the past few years?"

"Yeah, I could probably ballpark it," I deadpanned.

"Yes, of course, I'm sure you could," she said, giving me a small smile. "And for such a small town, it's a very disturbing number."

"And since we're so heavily dependent on tourists, any more bad press could be devastating to the local economy. I'm very familiar with the concept, Mom."

"Yes, I know you are, darling. But I've gotten several calls the past few days from journalists on both sides of the border who heard about what happened at the 147. They wanted quotes for articles they're writing about how dangerous it might be for people to visit our lovely little town. Can you think of anything worse?"

"A feature on 60 Minutes."

"Yes, there is that," she said, managing a small laugh. "Anyway, the Chief wants to talk with you to find out if you know anything that might help."

"I see." An evil grin appeared I wasn't proud of, but it refused to leave. I glanced off into the distance and hoped she didn't notice. "Now you want my help."

"No, we just want to know what you know," she said, her voice rising. "There's a difference."

"I don't see it, Mom."

"That's okay, darling. But by the time lunch is over, you will." She glanced up and waved. "There they are. Play nice."

Chief Abrams and Detective Williams walked the length of the dining room then sat down on either side of me. We exchanged casual greetings. The temperature around the table remained cool.

"You guys have any trouble getting through the door?" I said, glancing back and forth at both cops.

"So much for playing nice," my mother said, shaking her head.

"How much pain are you guys in?" I said.

"Pain?" the Chief said, frowning.

"Asking me for help has really gotta hurt," I said, taking a sip of water.

"I told you this was a bad idea," Detective Williams said to the Chief.

"Are you done?" the Chief said, glaring at me.

"For now. I suppose you want to pick my brain."

"Well, it certainly wasn't our first choice," Detective Williams said.

"Yeah, who knows where that thing has been," the Chief said.

"There's my Chief," I said, laughing. "Okay, I'll talk. But you guys go first."

The Chief and Detective Williams looked at each other, then nodded.

"To be honest, we don't have much," the Chief said. "But we both sort of like the other kayaker for it."

"Gordo?" I said, raising an eyebrow.

"Yeah, Gordo," the Chief said, apparently surprised I knew the guys' name.

"Why do you think he did it?" I said.

"We don't have a motive," he said, shaking his head. "We're coming at it from the opportunity angle. He was right next to the guy when he got shot."

107

"What about the possibility that somebody shot him from the pine trees?" I said, then glanced up as our server approached. "Hi, Jeffrey. How's it going?"

"Just great, Suzy. Hi, folks," he said, glancing around the table. "Do you know what you'd like?"

He took our orders then headed off. I focused on the cops and waited for an answer to my question.

"We've been going back and forth on that one," Detective Williams said. "But there's nothing to support the idea. And it would be a tough shot."

"There are probably hundreds of deer hunters within twenty miles of here who could make that shot," I said.

"You might be right," the detective said with a shrug. "But why would anybody go to all that trouble when it would have been so much easier to shoot him from the River?"

"There were a ton of people on the River the other day. Maybe the shooter was worried it would be too easy to spot him or his boat. Or he felt more comfortable on land," I said. "A lot of people just don't like being on boats. Maybe the shooter has never spent any time on the water before."

"I still like this guy Gordo for it," Detective Williams said, dismissing my ideas with a backhanded wave.

"Is he still in town?" I said.

"Yeah, we asked him to stick around for a few days," the detective said. "Along with all the folks staying at the Anderson place."

"Why would you do that?" I said, surprised.

"Primarily because they had a crappy attitude and annoyed me," Detective Williams said.

"They didn't want to talk to you, did they?" I said, glancing back and forth at the cops.

"No, they didn't," the Chief said.

"And?" I said, raising an eyebrow.

"And you were right about that," he whispered.

"Thank you," I said. "You didn't get anything out of them?"

"Nothing that would indicate any sort of motive," Detective Williams said. "Or any involvement on their part."

"Hmmm," I said, taking a sip of water.

"Okay, darling. That's enough. I don't handle coy very well on an empty stomach. Fess up."

"I've only got a couple of theories about the motive," I said, shrugging.

"That's two more than we've got," the Chief said. "Talk to me, Suzy."

"Well, one is jealousy. I'm pretty sure the dead guy, Charlie, had been having an affair with Emma."

"The woman who works for the clothing company?" Detective Williams said.

"That's the one. And her and Matisse have a strange relationship," I said. "My guess is that they've been an item for a while, but it's pretty clear it wasn't an exclusive arrangement."

"And she told you she had something going on with the victim?" the detective said.

"No, not directly," I said, shaking my head. "It was just a vibe I picked up on while I was there. It's probably something that only a *girl* would notice."

Detective Williams flinched at my shot across the bow, then reached for his water glass. He took a sip and a couple of deep breaths before continuing.

"Matisse is the guy from Montreal who works for the beer company, right?" the detective said.

"That's him," the Chief said. "I didn't like that guy at all. Arrogant and smug is such an ugly combination."

"They're synonyms, Chief," I said, glancing at him. "There's no need to use both."

"Don't start," my mother said.

"But I agree with you. Matisse is very annoying," I said. "And even though he and Emma seem to give each other a hard time about their indiscretions, it looked like it was some weird form of foreplay. But I don't think it has anything to do with the murder."

"Then why bring it up?" Detective Williams snapped.

"Because you really can't eliminate a theory until it's at least been formulated," I said, glaring at him. "Or didn't they teach you that at detective school?"

"Okay, darling," my mother said, reaching for a piece of bread. "Dial it down. You too, Detective."

"What's your other theory?" the Chief said.

"That Charlie's gambling problem was the reason why he got shot."

I let my comment hang like a cloud over the table while I reached for a piece of bread. I broke off a corner and dredged it in olive oil. Both cops stared at me while I chewed.

"Gambling problem?" the Chief said.

"Geez, you sound surprised, Chief," I said, breaking off another piece of bread. I glanced at my mother. "I think Chef Claire has added something to the olive oil dip. What is that, tarragon?" I took another bite and chewed, deep in thought. "No, I think it's a hint of Kalamata. Nice."

My mother shook her head and exhaled audibly.

"What sort of gambling problem are you talking about?" Detective Williams said.

111

"The problem of losing," I said.

"Are you saying this guy was in over his head with gambling debts?" the Chief said.

Several snarky retorts flashed through my mind, but I merely nodded.

"He owed at least half a million," I said. 'Or so I've been told."

"Told by who?" Detective Williams said.

"Whom."

The detective gripped the edge of the table with both hands. It was completely understandable. I was beginning to annoy myself.

"It was just something I heard when I was having lunch with them the other day," I said. "I don't remember who happened to mention it."

"Now, there's a motive," the Chief said. "I take it the guy didn't lose all that money in a casino."

"No, I imagine he didn't," I said.

"So, this guy ran up half a million in bad bets with a bookmaker who got tired of waiting for him to pay it back?" the detective said. "I don't know. Usually, those guys like to send a message before they take somebody out. He can't very well pay it back once he's dead."

"Maybe he'd already been warned," I said, deciding to toss my line into the water to see if I got a nibble. "Did the victim have some broken bones or anything like that?"

"Nothing. The guy was in perfect shape," the Chief said. "Which makes sense if you'd seen how fast he was in the water."

I let the Chief's comment sink in. He was absolutely right about that. Unless a previous wound had already healed.

"So, he didn't have any scars or marks that would indicate an old wound?" I said casually.

"No, he didn't," the Chief said, turning suspicious. "Why do you ask?"

"Just wondering," I said, shrugging. "Maybe the guy Charlie owed money to did something to him in the past, and he had healed up, but still not paid."

"No, there was nothing like that. Freddie checked him out very carefully."

The Chief continued to study me closely, and I eventually got annoyed.

"What are you staring at?"

"Did you hear any names about who Charlie had been placing his bets with?" the Chief said.

"Not a word," I said, shaking my head. Since I'd already told Rocco I'd be visiting Pizza Oven Paulie on my own, and he'd be sharing that tidbit with the gangster, there was no way I was going to divulge what I knew. "But that would probably be pretty useful information if you knew that, huh?"

"Yeah, it probably would," the Chief said, resuming his laser-like stare. "Why don't I believe you, Suzy?"

"Gee, I don't know, Chief," I said, shrugging. "But what can I say? I'm just a girl and not smart enough to help you out with the investigation."

"Darling, please. Let it go."

"No one said you weren't smart enough, Suzy," the Chief said, glancing at my mother. "It's just too dangerous for a civilian to be involved in this sort of thing."

"And yet here I am at lunch with two cops trying to find out what I know," I said. "Well, doesn't that just frost your cupcakes? Isn't that how you'd say it, Mom?"

"Why do I even worry about grandkids?" my mother said. "I already have a three-year-old daughter."

"So sorry to disappoint you," I snapped.

"Let's not do this again," she said, glaring at me. "At least not here. We'll head to my place after lunch to finish this discussion."

"I'm leaving," I said, getting up out of my chair. "Enjoy your lunch."

"Where on earth are you going?" she said.

"I think I'll take a nice long drive."

"Sit down and eat your lunch, young lady."

"Nice try, Mom," I said, rattling my car keys in front of her face. "But unfortunately for you, this three-year-old has her driver's license."

I stormed out of the dining room into the kitchen. Chef Claire noticed the look on my face and followed me toward the back door.

"What's the matter?" she said.

"Take a wild guess."

"Okay, I got it," she said, nodding. "Are you going home?"

"No."

"I'm heading home after lunch and taking the rest of the day off. I thought I'd grill some steaks. You will be home for dinner, right?"

"I'll let you know."

I slammed the door on my way outside then dialed Rocco's number. I headed across the parking lot toward my car as I waited for him to answer.

"Hey," Rocco said. "I was just about to call you."

"And?"

"I spoke with Paulie, and he agreed to meet with you."

"That's great," I said, climbing into the car and slamming the door. "Call him back and tell him I'm on my way."

"You're heading down there now?"

"Why not?"

"What's the matter with you?"

"It's nothing. I just went a couple more rounds with my mother."

"Are you okay?"

"I've got a couple of flesh wounds but nothing I can't handle. Just tell him I'll be there in about three hours. And get me the address of the place where he's going to be."

"Will do. I'll call you back."

"Thanks, Rocco."

"Suzy?"

"Yeah?"

"You're going to have a lot of time to cool off on the drive. I suggest you use it wisely. Do not, and I can't stress this enough, do not go into a meeting with Paulie Provincial with that attitude."

"I promise I'll be on my best behavior."

"Good. I just hope it's enough."

"Funny."

"Like I said last night, I wish I was joking."

Chapter 11

My route was simple, head south on Route 81, then pick up the Thruway west until I reached the exits for Rochester, a city on Lake Ontario I liked but didn't get a chance to visit often. Just outside of Clay Bay, I slid a Keith Jarrett CD into the player, and his solo piano eventually began to soothe my anger and bruised feelings.

The first thing I needed to do was get a handle on why I was acting the way I was. It certainly wasn't the first time my mother or the Chief had tried to curtail my level of involvement with an investigation, but this time seemed different. The intensity of their refusal to let me help had initially caught me by surprise, and I'd been wrong in thinking that their resolve would fade when confronted with my counter-arguments. And when their protests continued, I'd decided to conduct my own investigation just to prove to them how badly they needed my help.

As far as crime-solving strategies go, it probably wasn't my best effort. But on the petulant front, I'd hit a home run.

Now, I was pretty much on my own and had managed to annoy and offend the most important people in my life.

And I'd done it by being stubborn and snarky. Then, thirty miles outside of Rochester, I had a minor epiphany.

I suppose my mother might be right: Maybe I was acting like a three-year-old.

Before I had time to take a peek under that particular rug, mercifully, my phone rang. I slid my phone into its dashboard holder and answered.

"Where are you?" Josie said.

"I decided to go for a drive to cool off," I said, lowering the volume of the music.

"Is that Keith Jarrett I'm hearing?"

"Yeah."

"That's your thinking music," Josie said.

"It is."

"And?"

"And I've been thinking," I snapped.

"Okay," Josie said softly. "Let's start this conversation over. Are you all right?"

"I'm fine," I said, checking my mirrors then moving over into the slow lane.

"What happened at lunch? Chef Claire said you were off the planet when you left the restaurant."

"I'm just tired of being told to mind my own business then have them come to me for information the first time they get stuck."

"I see."

"Don't patronize me, Josie," I snapped. "And let's not forget that you took my mother's side."

"That's what this is about? The fact that I don't want to see you get shot?"

"It's about me being able to live my life without her constant interference. Sit up straight, *darling*. Don't talk with your mouth full. Wear something nice. Get married. Give me grandkids. I've had it."

"You forgot one," Josie whispered.

"What?" I snapped.

"Don't get shot."

"Funny."

"I wasn't going for funny," Josie said. "Suzy, your mother is just concerned about your safety. You're the one calling it meddling."

"So, you are taking her side," I said, taking my foot off the accelerator after I realized I'd sped up to ninety.

"Yes, I'm definitely in the *don't get shot* camp," she said. "If that puts me on your mother's side, guilty as charged."

120

"Why is my snooping all of a sudden a major problem?"

"Because you don't seem to have any boundaries anymore," Josie said softly. "At least when it comes to these investigations. Your mother and the Chief are worried that the law of averages is eventually going to catch up with you. And as much as you're going to hate what I'm about to say, I agree with them."

"I see."

"Petulant doesn't work with me, Suzy," Josie snapped. "Let's try adult for a while, shall we?"

"This conversation is over," I said, ending the call.

I turned the music back up and stared out at the highway. Fortunately, traffic was light, and I was able to wipe my eyes dry without causing an accident. A few minutes later, I called back.

"Sorry," I whispered when she answered.

"Forget it," Josie said. "Are you coming home for dinner? We're grilling steaks, and I made a nice salad."

"No, I'm in the mood for pizza," I said, lowering the music again.

"Pizza? Don't tell me you're going to C's to have a pizza."

"No, I'm going to try a new place," I said, realizing that my stomach was rumbling from having missed lunch.

"I haven't heard anything about a new pizza joint opening up," she said. "Where is it?"

"Are you going to tell my mother?"

"You don't want me to tell your mother about a new pizza place? Suzy, I think you're taking this feud thing a bit too far."

"Are you going to tell her or not?"

"No, it'll be our little secret," Josie said, laughing.

"It's in Rochester."

"You're driving to Rochester for pizza?"

"Yes."

"That's a long way to go for a slice," Josie said. "It must be good."

"I hear it's fantastic."

"Are we going to keep dancing, or are you ready to tell me the truth about what you're doing in Rochester? You know, just between you and me."

"It's related to the murder," I said. "I think I might have figured out a connection."

"Unbelievable," Josie whispered. "Just turn around and come home, Suzy. Please."

"I'll be fine," I said, checking the exit signs as I approached the outskirts of the city.

"Your mother has been looking for you all afternoon," Josie said.

"Well, now you'll be able to give her a call and put her mind at ease."

"Who are you meeting with down there?" Josie said.

"Oh, I'm getting another call," I said. "Gotta run."

I ended the call and answered the new one.

"Hey, Rocco," I said. "Thanks for calling me back."

"Paulie is at his new restaurant," Rocco said. "You got something to write with?"

"I do," I said, reaching for a pen. "He's got more than one restaurant?"

"He's got a bunch of them," he said, then recited the address. "He said he'll be waiting for you at his private table in the back."

"What did you tell him about me?"

"Just that you're a friend of mine who's trying to get some information."

"That's it?" I said, frowning.

"That's all I needed to say. The rest is up to you."

"Did you mention my mother?"

"I did not," Rocco said. "I thought it might be a good trump card to play just in case you end up needing it."

"Thanks, Rocco. I'll let you know how it goes."

"I wish I had a better feeling about this."

"You worry too much," I said, exiting the Thruway.

Chapter 12

I found the restaurant in a comfortable suburb on the outer edge of the city and parked in the crowded lot. My mood was better, but still not chirpy, and it worsened a bit as I walked toward the front door and remembered that I was about to sit down with a gangster who might have recently ordered the hit on the dead kayaker. The fact that he also used to date my mother didn't necessarily increase my anxiety level, but it was certainly doing a number on my curiosity.

I stepped inside and was overwhelmed by the smells of garlic and onion and freshly baked bread. My stomach rumbled again. I informed the hostess I was meeting Mr. Provincial, and she led me toward the back of the packed restaurant. On the way, we passed a massive brick pizza oven that was big enough to hold a dozen pies at one time. I snuck a quick peek for signs of handprints but came up empty. The hostess stopped in a doorway that led into a small room and gestured for me to enter. She left and closed the door behind her.

The man sitting in a booth set for two glanced up when I entered and studied me closely. He was somewhere in his sixties, and his salt and pepper hair was abundant but neatly trimmed. A pair of round, tortoiseshell glasses were perched on the bridge of his nose, and he wore a white dress shirt with the sleeves rolled up. If I had been given a guess, I would have gone with lawyer or accountant. And if there was a stereotype of what a gangster should look like, this guy wasn't it. Like my mother, he was aging gracefully, and it was easy to understand why she'd found him attractive. But I couldn't miss the intensity in his eyes or the way they bore into me. Then a huge smile appeared, and he waved me over.

"Suzy, right?" he said, standing briefly to extend his hand.

"Yes, it's so nice to meet you Mr. Provincial," I said, returning the handshake. "And thanks so much for agreeing to meet with me."

"Any friend of Rocco's is always welcome," he said, sitting down and gesturing for me to do the same. "Are you hungry?"

"Actually, I'm famished," I said, taking a seat in the chair fronting the red leather booth. "I missed lunch."

"Dealing with a busy day, huh?"

"Actually, I was dealing with a busybody," I said, shrugging. "My mother."

He laughed and gestured to one of the wait staff who was hovering nearby.

"I hope you like Italian," he said. "Jimmy, we'll start with some bread and an order of the roasted peppers."

"Yes, sir," the server said. "Would you like anything to drink?"

"Absolutely," he said, giving me the once-over. "I'm going to guess that you're a wine drinker."

"I am," I said, nodding. "But if we're having pizza, I'd prefer a beer."

"Good call," he said, nodding his approval. "Beer it is. Thanks, Jimmy."

"Yes, sir. I'll be right back."

"Okay, I'm all yours," Pizza Oven Paulie said.

He leaned back in his chair and dropped one arm below the table. It was now hidden from view by the large checkered tablecloth that hung low. I did my best not to stare and wonder about what sort of weapon he might be holding under the table.

"I'd like to talk with you about a guy named Charlie Viceroy," I said, leaning forward.

"Charlie? Sure, I know Charlie," he said, wary. "Just how much did Rocco tell you about my business?"

"I suppose you want me to be honest with you, right?"

"Let's just say, that if you weren't, I'd be…disappointed," he said, smiling.

"Sure, sure. Well, I know that you're a successful restauranteur," I said. "And I know that Rocco used to work for you in the past."

"But not making pizzas, right?" he said, studying me closely.

"No," I said, feeling my face flush. Then I shrugged it off and decided to play it completely straight with him. "I know a lot about Rocco's past, and since he used to work for you, Mr. Provincial, I have a pretty good idea about some of the things you're involved with."

"Used to be involved with," he said softly.

"Really?" I said, surprised.

"I've gotten out of most of the *unsavory* aspects of my previous life. These days, I pretty much focus on running my restaurants."

"They do take a lot of work," I said. "We have two. Fortunately, I don't have to spend a lot of time managing them."

"You have two restaurants? I'm impressed."

"Yes, we have one in Clay Bay. And the other is in Grand Cayman. That's the place Rocco manages for us."

"Rocco is managing a restaurant," he said, shaking his head. "My, how things change."

"He's really happy," I said, smiling. "And very good at what he does. But Rocco did happen to mention that you're still *dabbling* on the dark side."

"Dabbling on the dark side?" he said, laughing. "I'll need to remember that. I'm correct assuming you're not affiliated with law enforcement, right?"

"Absolutely not. In fact, we're barely on speaking terms at the moment."

I glanced over my shoulder when the server arrived with our beers and a plate of roasted peppers. He placed a basket of steaming fresh bread on the table, and I almost started salivating.

"Thanks, Jimmy," Paulie said, giving the peppers a loving stare. "And I think we'll have a large pie." He glanced at me. "How does pepperoni, sausage, and mushroom sound?"

"You read my mind, Mr. Provincial," I said, helping myself to the peppers and bread. I swallowed bites of both and immediately started to feel better. "These are fantastic."

The server left, and Paulie raised his beer glass in a toast. I clinked glasses and took a sip.

"Peroni, right?"

"A woman who knows her beer. Very good," he said, taking a long swallow. "So, Suzy, since you don't spend a lot of time running your restaurants, how do you keep yourself busy?"

"I run a doggy inn," I said, reaching for another piece of bread.

"Really? What does that entail?"

"We board dogs when their owners are away. And we run a huge rescue program. And my partner is a vet, so we offer a full range of services on that side of the business as well."

"How many dogs are we talking about?" Paulie said, stacking some of the peppers on top of a piece of bread.

"It varies," I said, shrugging. "But this morning's count was fifty-eight. Not counting the seven we have at the house."

"That's a lot of dogs," he said, laughing.

"You would think so, but not really," I said, shrugging. "But I do have to admit that having seven in the house is getting to be a bit much even for us."

"I assume they're small dogs," he said, quickly working his way through his first beer.

"No, they're all bruisers," I said, shaking my head. "I have an Australian Shepherd, my partner, Josie, has a

Newfie, and our other partner, Chef Claire, has two Goldens. And we recently acquired three young Labrador retrievers. There's never a dull moment."

"I love big dogs," he said. "Especially Labs. And even more so, this guy." He pulled the tablecloth back to reveal a black lab that was stretched out on the booth with its head in his lap. "This is Mercury."

So much for my concern that the guy was pointing a handgun at me under the table. I got up out of my chair and slid into the booth next to the dog. I scratched his back leg, and the dog seemed to sigh as he lifted his head to look at me.

"He's gorgeous," I said, sitting back down in my chair.

"He's a great dog," Paulie said, his hand sliding back down below the table. "But he's getting up there. He just turned ten. I've been thinking about getting another one. A young one. You know, a playmate to help keep Mercury active and young at heart."

"It's a good strategy to use for older dogs," I said, nodding. "And it usually works well."

He finished his beer, then focused on what was left of the peppers.

"So, you're a full-time dog lover and a quasi-involved restauranteur."

"Yeah, that pretty much sums it up," I said, taking a sip.

"But you want to talk with me about my *dabbling*?" he said, raising an eyebrow.

"Yes, sir, I would."

"I assume Charlie is a friend of yours?

"No, I never even met the guy," I said.

"Okay, now I'm officially confused," he said.

"Yeah, I really need to start working on that," I said, finishing the last of my beer. "I'm here to see if I can find anything out about his gambling debts that might be useful."

"Useful for what?" Paulie said, scowling.

"To figure out who shot him."

Paulie flinched, then sat back in the booth. He stared across the table at me, and it was pretty obvious it was news to him.

"Charlie's dead?" he said softly.

"Yeah. He got shot in the back. My guess is that it was a rifle shot from about three hundred yards."

"That's awful," he said, glancing down at the table. "I always liked Charlie."

"Even though he owed you a half million?" I said, dredging a piece of bread through the final drops of oil on the pepper plate.

"Charlie didn't owe me a half a million. In fact, he didn't owe me anything."

"He didn't?" I said, frowning.

"No. He did get pretty far behind about a year ago, but we had a little chat, and he took care of it. Since then, we never had any problems with his account," Paulie said. "Where did you hear he owed me money?"

"From some of his friends," I said, my neurons flaring.

"Some friends," he said, shrugging. "Oh, good. There's our pie."

The server set an enormous pizza down on the table as well as two fresh beers. After checking to make sure we had everything we needed, he excused himself and left us by ourselves. Paulie placed a steaming hot slice on my plate, then served himself. I shook red chili flakes onto my slice and took a bite.

"Oh, my word," I said, staring at him. "This is the best pizza I've ever had in my life."

I hoped that Chef Claire would forgive me for saying it, but it was. I took another bite and savored it.

"This is magnificent. How do you do it?" I said.

"It's in the water," he said. "I'm glad you like it." He took another bite and caught my eye while he chewed. "You thought I might have arranged a hit on Charlie?"

I swallowed hard and killed a little time by taking a sip of beer.

"Yeah, I thought it might be a possibility. As soon as I heard he owed a lot of money and that you were his bookie, I sort of put two and two together," I said, choosing my words carefully.

"And came up with five?" he said, reaching across the table.

I flinched and closed my eyes expecting the worst. Then I realized he was merely picking a long string of mozzarella off my chin.

"Thanks," I said, wiping my face. "Just so you know, Rocco told me I was nuts to think that you might have been involved."

"I don't know why he would," Paulie said, shrugging. "It's certainly something I might have considered in the past. I assume you've heard the story about how I got my nickname."

"I did hear something in passing about that," I said, reaching for another slice. "Is it true?"

"No, it's total folklore," Paulie said, shaking his head. "I was in one of my old pizza joints having a chat with this guy about paying what he owed me, and he got scared and tried to run. On his way out, he slipped on the tile floor and tried to catch his balance and just happened to grab the side of the oven. I wouldn't waste my pizza oven on some lousy gambler."

"Not to mention what it might do to the taste of the pizza."

"Exactly," he said, laughing. "You're funny."

"Thanks. But I know several people who'd probably disagree with you," I said, taking a huge bite out of my slice. "This is remarkable pizza, Mr. Provincial." I chewed and let my neurons churn for a few moments. Eventually, they settled down. "The one time that Charlie got behind. How much did he owe you?"

"I think it was somewhere around two hundred thousand," he said. "After that, he actually set up an account with me and made a huge deposit just so he never went into the red. That's probably where the half a million number came from."

"He kept a half million bucks in his gambling account?" I said, frowning.

"Give or take. It would fluctuate based on how he was doing," Paulie said. "The guy would bet on anything. I'd get calls from all over the world from him. I could never figure out exactly what he did for a living?"

"He was a professional athlete," I said, polishing off the last of my second slice. "Water events. Swimming, kayaking, stuff like that. Apparently, he competed all over the world. And he also had some endorsement deals."

"Interesting," he said, reaching for another slice. "I guess I'm going to have to figure out what to do with the balance in his account."

"How much is in there?"

Paulie grabbed a notepad from his pocket and flipped through the pages until he located the one he was looking for.

"Four hundred and sixty thousand and change," he said, sliding the notepad back into his shirt.

"You know, a lot of people are using computers for stuff like that these days," I said, nodding at the pad in his pocket.

"Yeah, and a lot of those people are sitting in jail," he said, smiling at me. "The Feds are good, but I'd like to see them try to hack into my notebook."

"It's hard to argue with your logic," I said, nodding as I reached for yet another slice. "Where do you think Charlie got all his money?"

"I have no idea," Paulie said. "Maybe he won it from somebody else. Or stole it."

"Can I ask you a question?"

"Now, you suddenly feel the need for permission?" he said, grinning at me over the rim of his glass.

"This one might make you mad."

"If I was going to get mad, you'd have noticed by now," he said, giving me a look that made the hairs on the back of my neck stand up. "Go ahead and ask your question."

"I'm just wondering why you're still involved in bookmaking. It's pretty obvious that you're doing very well with your restaurants."

"My ex-wife used to ask me the same question all the time," he said, shrugging. "Like you say, I'm only *dabbling* these days. Just to keep the juices flowing. The restaurants are doing great, but there's not a lot of excitement compared to the old days. And I've never liked the thought of the government telling people they can't do something they enjoy. If somebody wants to put a few bucks down on their favorite team, isn't that their business?"

"So, you're providing some sort of public service?" I said, setting my slice down to catch my breath.

"Yeah, a public service. That's what I'm doing," he said, nodding. Then he frowned and shook his head. "Poor Charlie. I can't believe he got shot."

"Would you like me to see if I can find out who should get the money in his account?" I said.

"That would be good. I wouldn't know where to start. Would you like another beer?"

"No, thanks, two's my limit," I said.

"I'm that way with martinis," he said. "It's like Dorothy Parker used to say."

I grinned when I remembered the quote my mother often referenced. "I like martinis, but I have to stop at two. After three, I'm under the table."

"And after four, I'm under the host," he said, laughing as he finished the quote. "That Parker quote was the favorite of someone I used to date." Then he stared at me for a long time until I grew uncomfortable.

"What are you looking at?" I said, glancing down to check if I'd spilled something on myself.

"I knew you looked familiar," he said softly. "Don't tell me that she's your mother."

"Yes, she is," I said, nodding.

"Suzy Chandler. Well, doesn't that just frost your cupcakes? I can't believe it."

"I couldn't believe it at first either when Rocco told me."

"But you decided not to tell me you knew about me and your mother?" he said, frowning.

138

"I wasn't sure it was relevant," I said, shrugging. "And I didn't want to make you uncomfortable."

"Or mad, right?" he said, grinning.

"Yeah, that thought did cross my mind. When did you two date?"

"It was a long time ago," he said, staring off into the distance. "We started seeing each other about a year after your dad died."

"You must have been the first man she dated," I said, searching my memory bank.

"I think I was."

"So, what happened?"

"She couldn't get past what I did for a living back then. And she was worried about putting her little girl in another difficult situation," he said. "That would be you, in case you're keeping score."

"Got it," I said as another wave of guilt washed over me.

"I should have gotten out of some of the things I was doing before she called it off. Who knows how things might have turned out. How is she doing?"

"Apart from being incredibly annoyed with me at the moment, she's doing really well."

"She's mad because you came down here to see me?" Paulie said, frowning.

"No, she doesn't know I'm here. But I suppose it couldn't hurt to tell her, right?"

"I don't see why it would. Please, send her my best."

"I'll do that," I said.

"Wow, talk about your full circle kind of night," he said. "Your mother is a real blast from the past. She's amazing."

"She has her moments."

He drifted off for a moment, then shook his head and looked at me.

"You know, if it wasn't for Charlie, I never would have opened my new place."

"It's very nice," I said, glancing around as I reached for my slice.

"No, I'm talking about my new place in Mexico. Charlie was always complaining about how he couldn't find decent pizza in this tourist town he liked to visit. I think it was one of his favorite spots to surf. He said I'd make a killing if I opened a place down there. Based on what we've seen so far, it looks like he might have been right."

"Punta Chicado?"

"Yeah," he said, surprised. "How the heck did you know that?"

"Lucky guess."

Chapter 13

I didn't get home until after midnight. There were so many thoughts bouncing around my head vying for my attention I purposely stayed below the speed limit just to be on the safe side. I entered through the kitchen and did my best not to make any noise, but was greeted by all seven dogs before I could even get the door closed. I knelt down and said hello to them then headed for the living room that was bathed in light. Josie and Chef Claire were lounging and watching a movie. I tossed my coat on a chair then settled down on one of the couches and waited for Chloe to get settled on my lap.

"Hey," Josie said. "We were just about to send out a search party. Are you okay?"

"I'm fine," I said. "And I'm sorry about giving you such a hard time earlier. I was acting like a spoiled brat."

"Acting?" Josie deadpanned.

"Don't start," I said, laughing. "Hi, Chef Claire."

"Hey. We're glad you're home," she said, putting the movie on pause. "Are you hungry?"

"No, I'm still stuffed," I said. "I think I ate the world's best pizza tonight."

"Really?" Chef Claire said. "We'll need to take a road trip."

"It was incredible," I said.

"Okay, Snoopmeister," Josie said, sitting up and tucking her legs underneath her. "Spill the beans. Why the need to drive all the way to Rochester?"

"To meet with the pizzamaker," I said, rubbing Chloe's head.

Josie and Chef Claire exchanged blank stares then looked back at me and waited.

"He was the dead guy's bookie," I said. "And one of my mother's old boyfriends."

"What on earth are you talking about?" Josie said.

"It's complicated," I said. "But I do need to tell Chief about it in the morning."

"Tell me what?" the Chief said as he entered the living room from the bathroom.

"What are you doing here?" I said, surprised to see him.

"Enjoying the company of these two amazing women, if you must know," he said.

"Aren't you sweet," Josie said, beaming at him.

"And since I was already here, I thought I'd just hang around and wait for you to get home. And before you ask,

142

your mother had nothing to do with it. I came over all on my own."

"I'm so sorry for my behavior at lunch, Chief," I said, getting up to give him a hug.

He squeezed me tight then grabbed my shoulders.

"Don't worry about it. I could have handled it a bit better myself. But your mother has been pretty adamant on this one. And in case you haven't noticed, she scares the crap out of me."

"The trick is to not show any fear," I said.

"Easy for you to say," he said, laughing. "Now, why don't you tell us about your trip?"

"I had to meet a guy," I said, remembering my promise to Rocco not to involve the cops.

"Hot date?" the Chief deadpanned.

"No, it wasn't a date. It was just a meeting."

"With who?"

"Whom."

The Chief did a slow burn but said nothing.

"I can't tell you, Chief," I said, shrugging. "I made a promise not to mention his name to the police."

"I see," he said. "So, you were meeting with a guy who's worried about the cops. Why doesn't that make me feel better?"

"I'm too tired to do rhetorical, Chief," I said, stretching back out on the couch.

"Well, can you at least tell me what you were talking about?"

"I can do that," I said. "I told you that I heard that Charlie, the guy who got shot, had a gambling problem. So I went to Rochester to meet with his bookie."

"But you chose not to mention you were planning on doing that at lunch?"

"I was trying to prove a point," I said.

"The point about how much smarter you are than the rest of us?" the Chief said, his voice rising.

"Let's not do this, okay?" Josie said, then glanced at Chief Abrams. "Just let her tell the story."

"Thank you," I said, nodding at Josie.

"You're welcome," she said, nodding back. "But don't start getting snarky. I'd like to get to bed at some point tonight."

"After I heard that Charlie owed his bookie a ton of money, I thought somebody might have put a contract out on him. But it turns out that Charlie didn't owe the guy anything. In fact, he had a gambling account with the bookie that has over four hundred thousand in it."

"Where did a guy who races kayaks for a living get his hands on that kind of money?" the Chief said.

"No idea," I said, shaking my head. "He certainly didn't make anywhere near that in prize money. Maybe his endorsements paid a lot more than I thought."

"Half a million to endorse beachwear and surfboards?" the Chief said, frowning.

"I guess it's possible," Josie said.

"Man, I'm in the wrong line of work," he said. "So, if the bookie didn't have any reason to kill him, what's the motive?"

"It has to be something related to Paddles," I said, tossing the idea out just to get it on the table. It had been rolling around inside my head since I'd left Rochester, and it was time to let somebody else deal with it for a while. "Maybe Charlie was stealing from Julian's company."

"The guy didn't even work there," the Chief said.

"I know. But he did have an endorsement deal with them. Maybe he was working with somebody on the inside," I said.

"You said you thought he was having an affair with Emma," the Chief said. "No wait, she works for the clothing company."

"Yeah, I couldn't make the connection, either," I said. "I'm missing something."

"You're sure the guy you met with in Rochester isn't involved?" the Chief said.

"I don't think he is," I said. "He seemed genuinely surprised when I told him Charlie was dead. And I believed him when he told me that he'd left his old life behind. These days, the only things he seems to worry about are his dogs and maintaining the quality of his pizza."

"Hey, wait a second," the Chief said, staring at me. "Don't tell me you had a meeting with Pizza Oven Paulie."

Caught red-handed and stunned, I stared at the Chief. Eventually, I slowly nodded.

"Yeah, I had dinner with Paulie Provincial."

"Pizza Oven Paulie," the Chief said, shaking his head. "I can't believe it."

"You know him?"

"Hey, I spent twenty years with the state police. All the cops know who Paulie is. I heard a rumor he's gone straight."

"Apart from the bookmaking, I think he has," I said. "How did you figure that out?"

"If you put Rochester, bookmaking, pizza, and dogs together, he's the only person you could possibly be talking about."

"I liked him," I said. "But you can't get him involved in this, Chief. I gave my word."

"To who?"

"Whom."

"Suzy, just let one go once in a while," Josie said.

"Sorry," I said. "I really don't want to get him in trouble. Wouldn't the cops move in if they heard that Paulie was still taking bets?"

"I'm sure the cops know what Paulie's doing," the Chief said. "But with everything else they have to worry about these days, I doubt very much they care about some illegal betting. And I'm sure Paulie has enough of the right palms greased."

"How about you, Chief?" Josie said, grinning. "You ever get your palms greased?"

"Hey, the only grease I ever got on my hands was from one of his slices," the Chief said, laughing. "The man sure knows his pizza."

"Is the other kayaker still around?" I said.

"Gordo?" the Chief said. "Yeah, he's still holed up in the hotel. Why do you want to know?"

147

"I thought I might swing by and talk to him about what Paulie should do with the four hundred thousand in Charlie's account," I said casually.

"And?" the Chief said.

"And nothing. But if Charlie had any family, they should probably get that money, right?"

"I suppose," the Chief said. "Maybe I should tag along."

"And then you could come up with an excuse to swing by the Anderson place and have another chat with the folks there," I said.

"I'd love to do that," the Chief said. "But they all left town today."

"I thought you asked them to stick around for a few days," I said.

"I did. But I didn't have enough of a reason to make them stay," the Chief said. "And I got a call from one of the CEO's lawyers reminding me of that fact."

"They're all gone?" I whispered.

"Almost all," Josie said.

I glanced over and waited for her to continue.

"Maria dropped off the Maltese at the Inn today. She said she was leaving the country for a few days and couldn't take the dog with her."

"She's going to Mexico," I said. "Punta Chicado."

"Is that supposed to mean something to me?" the Chief said.

"It's the town where Paddles has its factory," I said, sitting up on the couch. "That's going to make things a bit more difficult."

"What?" Chief Abrams said.

"Nothing," I said, flashing him a quick smile. "So, what time do you want to meet in the morning?"

Chapter 14

The man named Gordo answered our knock and nodded for us to follow him out onto the balcony that overlooked the River. He was barefoot, wearing shorts and a hooded sweatshirt and looked like he hadn't slept since the race three days ago. As I crossed the room, I noticed the trophy he'd received for winning the 147 sitting on a table next to the TV. Instead of being prominently displayed, the trophy was serving as a hat rack for a black fedora. Gordo sat down, gestured for us to do the same, and fixed his stare on a massive ship that was heading downriver toward the Atlantic.

"What a gorgeous view. I've spent the past few days sitting out here watching all the ships go by," Gordo said, his eyes still focused on the water. "I've probably seen a dozen different flags. But I don't recognize that one."

I glanced out at the ship's stern and saw the red and green flag with a coat of arms where the two colors met flapping in the breeze.

"Portugal," I said. "It's a Saltie."

"Saltie as in oceangoing?" Gordo said, reaching for his cup of coffee.

150

"Yes, as opposed to a Laker," I said. "Those are the ships that just travel the St. Lawrence and Great Lakes."

"Cool."

"I'm sorry about what happened to Charlie," I said.

Gordo shrugged and glanced at Chief Abrams.

"Did you stop by to tell me I'm free to leave?" he said.

"I can't think of any reason why you can't leave," the Chief said.

"You mean you don't have any reason to arrest me, right, Chief?" Gordo said, refilling his coffee. "You guys want coffee or something to eat? The room service here is pretty good."

We both declined the offer.

"Would you mind if I asked you a few questions?" I said.

"Go right ahead. You're actually the first one who's asked for permission."

"You and Charlie were good friends, right?"

"Best friends. Charlie was the best friend I ever had."

"And you traveled together all over the world to different events?"

"Yeah," he said, slowly nodding his head. "We went through a lot of stuff together."

"Do you know any reason why somebody would want to kill him?" I said.

"What is it with you people?" Gordo said, finally taking his eyes off the view to look at us. "You just keep asking the same questions hoping I'll eventually give you a different answer? You cops are unbelievable."

"Actually, I'm not a cop," I said.

Gordo gave me the once-over then frowned.

"Then why are you here asking me a bunch of questions?"

"He does have a point," the Chief whispered.

I shot him a dirty look then refocused on Gordo.

"I'm just trying to find out who should get the money in Charlie's gambling account," I said, unable to come up with a better response.

"His gambling account," Gordo said, shaking his head with a sad smile. "I always called it his illegal credit line. Do you know how much is in it at the moment?"

"In the neighborhood of half a million," I said.

Gordo barely reacted to the number.

"He said he'd been on a hot streak lately. All that money should go to his mom," Gordo said. "Do you know how to get in touch with her?"

"We found her contact information in his personal belongings," the Chief said. "She lives in California, right?"

"Yeah. And I'm sure she can use the money," Gordo said. "I spoke with her the night he got killed. She's devastated. Has his body been shipped to her yet?"

"I believe it has," the Chief said.

"So, you don't know who might have killed him?" I said.

Gordo exhaled loudly and shook his head in disgust.

"For the hundredth time, no, I don't," he said. "Is there anything else? I need to pack and hit the road."

"Where's your next event?" I said.

"There's no event. I'm taking a month off and heading to New Zealand to visit some friends," he said. "But I have a few things to take care of in Mexico first."

I glanced at Chief when he mentioned Mexico and my neurons flared. But they remained directionless, and I looked out at the River trying to remember what else I wanted to ask him.

"You both had endorsement deals with Paddles and Wet Water Fashions, right?" I said, then my face flushed. "But you still do, of course. I mean, your deals are still in place. I'm sorry. That must have sounded insensitive."

"We did," Gordo said. "What about them?"

153

"They must be big," I said. "I mean, for Charlie to be able to leave half a million just sitting around."

Gordo snorted.

"You're joking, right?" he said. "It's not like we could dunk or throw a football seventy yards. We were just a couple of paddleboard and kayak guys. Both deals together totaled two hundred grand. And we split 50/50. They're nice deals, but it's not exactly walking away money."

"Then where did Charlie get his gambling money?" I said.

"I imagine he must have been moonlighting," Gordo said, staring back out at the water. "Don't even bother asking me what he was doing."

"Because you don't know, or aren't going to tell me?" I said.

"Maybe you should have been a cop," Gordo said, glancing over at me. "You really are annoying."

"Sure, sure," I said. "So, are you going to answer the question?"

Gordo stared at me, then glanced over at the Chief.

"Are we about done here?" he said.

"Yeah, we're done," the Chief said, getting up out of his chair.

I started to protest then took a deep breath as I remembered the promise I'd made to myself about trying to play nicer with others. I stood and extended my hand.

"Thanks for your time, Gordo," I said. "We'll get in touch with Charlie's mother and arrange for the money to be sent to her. And I'm so sorry about what happened. Hopefully, the police will find Charlie's killer soon so you can get some closure."

"Yeah, good luck with that," Gordo said, returning my handshake without getting up from his chair.

We left him sitting there staring out at the River and let ourselves out. On our way down the hall toward the elevators, the Chief chuckled.

"Because you don't know, or aren't going to tell me?" he said, coming to a stop in front of the elevator and pushing the down button.

"Pretty smooth, huh?" I said, frowning. "I probably could have handled that one a bit better."

"Oh, I don't know," he said. "It certainly got his attention."

"It did, didn't it?"

The elevator arrived, and we stepped inside. I leaned against the back wall as the elevator began its descent.

"So, what do you think?" I said.

"About Gordo?" the Chief said. "I don't like him for the murder."

"Me neither," I said. "They were obviously best buddies."

"Yeah, the guy is definitely grieving."

"He is," I said, as the elevator came to a stop. "But I also picked up on something else."

"Me too," he said, making eye contact. "You go first."

"I think our guy Gordo is jonesing for a little revenge," I said, walking out of the elevator.

"Great minds think alike," he said, following me outside to the parking lot.

"Make sure you tell my mother that."

"You go first."

"Coward."

"Absolutely."

Chapter 15

I said goodbye to the Chief and headed for home. I parked in the driveway and walked down the path to the Inn and entered through the back door. Several dogs noticed my arrival immediately and began wagging their tails waiting for me to stop by their condo to say hello. I spent the next fifteen minutes making my way through the condo area greeting all of them, and by the time I entered the reception area, I was in a fantastic mood.

It works every time.

Josie was behind the registration counter reviewing the day's schedule with Sammy and Jill, and they all looked up when I approached.

"It's pretty quiet," I said, glancing around the empty waiting area.

"We had a big rush this morning," Jill said. "But the afternoon schedule is light."

"I was thinking about taking the afternoon off," Josie said. "You feel like taking the boat out? You can waste a couple hours trying to catch a fish while I read my book."

"For the record, I catch fish all the time," I said, making a face at her. "But I think I'll pass. I've got a ton of

157

paperwork to deal with, and I need to make sure payroll is ready to go."

"Then I'll just head up to the house and play with the dogs," Josie said. "Should we cook tonight, or just go to C's?"

"Let's just go to the restaurant," I said, then glanced at Sammy and Jill. "You guys want to join us?"

"Twist my arm," Sammy said, laughing.

"Yeah, I think we can make that work," Jill said. "Thanks. That sounds like fun. What time should we be there?"

"Seven?" I said, glancing at Josie.

"Perfect," Josie said, heading for the back door. "I'll see you guys later."

"How's the Maltese doing?" I said.

"She's great," Sammy said. "Nothing seems to rattle that dog. When I took her out to the condo yesterday, a dozen dogs gave her the once-over, and she just sat there quietly the whole time."

I headed back into the condo area and found the Maltese sitting on her bed. Her face was propped up on her front paws, and she stared at me with those big round eyes as soon as I entered. I gently lifted her off the bed, tucked her under my arm, and headed for my office. I set her down on top of my desk, and she immediately sat down and glanced around. Then she resumed the same pose she'd had in her condo, and I laughed.

"You really are Mellow, aren't you?" I said, scratching the top of her head.

I pulled a stack of papers out of one of the desk drawers and started working my way through them. After I finished reviewing those that needed attention and tossing the rest into the wastebasket, I grabbed my checkbook and began working my way through our monthly bills. Then I called the company that handled our payroll and confirmed the totals with them. I tossed my phone into my bag and glanced up at the clock and noticed that two hours had passed since I'd sat down. The Maltese continued to sit quietly on top of the desk, watching me as I worked. I returned all the paperwork to the drawer then sat back in my chair. I patted my leg, and the Maltese got up and hopped from the desk then took a few seconds to get settled on my lap. I looked down at the dog who yawned then lowered her head onto her front paws.

"What's your secret, Mellow?"

The dog cocked her head and glanced up at me. Then I heard the office door open, and my mother strolled in and sat down on the couch.

"Hi, Mom," I said.

159

"Hello, darling," she said. "What a cute dog. Wait a minute. Is that the same Maltese you found on the River the other day?"

"Yes, it is. This is Mellow."

"Please don't tell me you stole that woman's dog," my mother deadpanned.

"Mom, I've made the decision to try and be nicer to you," I said, my voice rising. "Please, don't make it harder."

"I was just joking. Where on earth has your sense of humor gone?"

"What can I do for you, Mom?"

"I just stopped by to apologize."

"For what?" I said, frowning.

"What do you mean, for what?"

"Well, there are so many things on the list," I said, raising an eyebrow in her direction.

"Okay," she said, nodding. "Are we even now?"

"Close enough," I said, shrugging.

"What do you want me to do, darling?" she said. "Please, tell me because I'm out of ideas."

"You could start by trying not to interfere."

"I suppose I could try. What do you have in mind?"

"How about laying off the grandkids comments?" I said. "I'm probably more worried about it than you are, and your constant harping isn't helping."

"Okay, fair enough," she said, draping a leg over her knee. "What else can I do?"

"Back off on giving the Chief such a hard time," I said. "I know you're only doing it to get me under control, but he's about to crack from the pressure you're putting on him. Just leave him alone, and let him do his job."

"I didn't realize he was having such a hard time with my *suggestions*," she said, glancing around the office.

"He's one of the best things that's ever happened to this town," I said. "But if you keep it up, he's going to decide it's not worth the abuse and retire."

"Abuse? That's a bit harsh, wouldn't you say?"

"Yeah, it probably is. Sorry."

"I have been hard on him," she said, nodding. "But I couldn't come up with any other way to control your tendencies."

"Just deal with me directly and leave him out of it," I said. "I'm making my own decisions, Mom. And in case you haven't noticed, I'm good at this stuff."

"All right, darling. I'll back off. And I should probably apologize to him as well."

"I'm sure he and his blood pressure will thank you."

"What else?"

"I want you to stop doing everything you can to keep me from helping out with these investigations," I said firmly.

"That's asking a lot," she said, shaking her head.

"I'll make you a deal," I said. "You agree to stay out of it for a year, and I promise I'll do everything I can to find someone to settle down with."

I stared out the window and rubbed the sleeping Maltese's head.

"You're serious?" my mother said.

"Yes, it's time for me to start seriously thinking about having a family," I said, nodding.

My mother studied me closely with a confused look on her face.

"Why the sudden change of heart?"

"It's not really that sudden," I said. "I've been thinking about it for a while. But I had a conversation last night that got me thinking about choices and decisions."

"I see," she said. "Those can be very tough questions to deal with."

"Indeed," I said. "And after that conversation, I came to a conclusion, that after all the decisions you've made on my behalf, I owe you one."

"Only one?"

"Please, don't start, Mom."

"Sorry. But I think I'm going to need a bit more, darling," she said, leaning forward on the couch.

"I had dinner with an old friend of yours last night."

"Really? Is that where you went on your drive?"

"It was," I said. "I had dinner with Paulie Provincial."

My mother sat back on the couch like I'd punched her. And from a memory bank perspective, I suppose I had.

"Why would you have dinner with Paulie?" she said, wide-eyed. "And how on earth did you know we were friends?"

"Long story," I said, shrugging.

"Don't worry, I'll make time."

I spent a few minutes telling her the story, and she listened closely. When I finished, I sat back in my chair and waited for her to respond.

"How is he doing?" she said softly.

"He's great," I said. "I like him a lot."

"Yes, so do I," she said, her eyes watering.

For the second time in a few short days I'd made my mother cry, and I felt lower than a garden slug wearing a backpack. I handed her a box of tissues, and she spent a few minutes recovering.

163

"Oh, my," she said, tossing a used tissue into the trash. "Where on earth did that come from?"

"I'm going to ask you something, Mom, and I need you to be honest with me."

"Go ahead," she whispered.

"You broke things off with Paulie because you were worried about what he did for a living, and the impact it would have had on me if he'd gotten shot or gone to jail, right?"

She wiped her eyes briefly then looked at me and gave me a small nod.

"Nothing gets past you."

"You didn't have to do that, Mom," I said, crushed that I'd been the reason she'd ended the relationship. "I'm sure I could have handled whatever happened."

"I just couldn't take the chance you'd have to go through a loss like that again. You'd just lost your father the year before," she said, exhaling loudly. "I felt it was the only decision I could make at the time. Especially after Paulie refused to get out of some of the things he was involved with."

"Well, he's out now," I said.

"So I've heard," she said, brushing her hair away from her face.

"Really?"

"I have my sources," she said, giving me a small smile. "But I haven't seen Paulie in years."

"He looks fantastic. And he's single at the moment."

"That I did not know," she said, cocking her head. "Did you eat at one of his restaurants?"

"Yes, at his new place out in the suburbs."

"Did you have pizza?"

"We did."

"Best I ever had," she said, nodding. "The pizza was pretty good, too."

"Mom!"

"Relax, darling," she said, laughing. "I'm just having a little fun with you." She relaxed and again draped a leg over her knee. "You're convinced he didn't have anything to do with the murder of the kayaker?"

"I'm positive."

"Do you have any idea who did?" she said.

"I have a working theory," I said. "But I'm going to need to do a little more digging."

"Of course, you are," she said, shaking her head. "Okay, darling, I'll agree to back off. But if I don't see some serious traction on the dating front very soon, we're going to be revisiting this issue."

"Fair enough," I said, gently lifting the Maltese off my lap and placing her on the desk. I stood up and sat down next to my mother and gave her a long hug.

"I love you, Mom."

"Love you, too, darling," she said, returning my embrace then getting to her feet. "What's your next move?"

"I thought I might give eHarmony a shot," I deadpanned.

"You know what I'm talking about," she said, glaring at me.

"Oh, that," I said, grinning at her. "Well, I need to talk to the Chief and Detective Williams, but I do have an idea."

She stared at me and waited.

"I'm thinking about taking a little vacation."

"Vacation? I wouldn't have gotten that with a hundred guesses," she said, frowning. "Vacation where?"

"Mexico," I said, turning coy. "Say, why don't you give Paulie a call and invite him along? It would be a great place for the two of you to reconnect. You know, a little time in the sun, frosty margaritas, long walks on the beach."

"*You're* trying to fix *me* up?"

"Yeah, how do you like it?" I said, beaming at her.

"Actually, darling," she said, her eyes twinkling. "It's not the worst idea you've ever had."

"It's not?" I said, stunned.

"It doesn't even crack the top ten," she said, getting to her feet. "I need to run, but I'll be in touch. And please be careful, darling."

"Sure, sure."

She shook her head then gently placed a hand on my cheek and patted it lovingly.

"You are something else," she said, then reached down to scratch the Maltese's head. "Is the dog always this calm and relaxed?"

"Yeah, I think she is."

"What's her secret?"

Chapter 16

"Suzy?"

"Yeah?"

"I'm going to need that arm in good working condition."

"Sorry, Chief," I said, glancing down and removing my fingernails from his forearm. "I get a little nervous when I fly."

The Chief rubbed his arm and the four imprints I'd left slowly began to fade.

"I can't believe I let you talk me into this," he said, glancing out the window as the private jet rose into the air.

"Having you tag along was the only way my mother would agree to let me go," I said, taking a few deep breaths as the plane continued its ascent.

"So, now I'm tagging along?"

"You know what I mean," I said. "What are they doing back there?"

The Chief glanced over his shoulder where my mother and Paulie were sitting a few rows back.

"It looks like they're snuggling," he said. "Weird. I can't believe I'm flying to Mexico on a private jet with Pizza Oven Paulie."

"What did your wife say when you told her you were going to Mexico with me?" I said, sneaking a peek over my shoulder.

"Before or after she started laughing?"

"It's not that funny," I said, frowning. "If we had to, I suppose we could pass as a couple."

"A couple of what?" he said, glancing over at me.

"Good point. Anyway, thanks for agreeing to come along."

"Are you sure Paulie has enough room for us at his place?" the Chief said.

"I guess," I said, shrugging. "All he said was that he'd bought a bungalow on the beach in Punta Chicado. What's the matter, Chief? Worried that we're going to have to share a room?"

"Terrified."

"Funny."

"Are we going to get a chance to do a little deep-sea fishing?" he said.

"Maybe."

"How long are we going to be gone?"

"I don't know."

"What do you expect to find down there?"

"I have no idea."

"I'm glad you've got the plan all worked out," the Chief said.

"Don't start," I said, punching him gently on the shoulder. "I had no idea my mother was going to jump all over the idea to come down here. I haven't had time to come up with a plan. I figured we'd just work on it during the flight."

"Okay, let's start with the factory," the Chief said.

"What about it?" I said, finally relaxing as the plane leveled off. I unfastened my seatbelt and stretched my back.

"Are you just planning on popping in for a visit? You know, give them the old, we were just in the neighborhood and thought we'd stop by to say hi?"

"That would be pretty hard to explain," I said, reaching into my satchel for a bag of bite-sized. I offered the Chief the bag, and he waved it off.

"Probably not any harder to explain than it's going to be if they ask us what we're doing in Punta Chicado."

"Oh, I've got that one all figured out," I said. "Paulie is our out on that question. He decided to check up on his new restaurant down here and invited us along."

"That's not bad," the Chief said, then frowned. "Hey, was that your plan from the start, or did you just happen to

170

come up with the Paulie angle after your mom talked him into coming along?"

"After," I said, popping a bite-sized into my mouth.

"That's good," the Chief said. "Because if that was your idea right from the jump, that would have been way too Machiavellian. Even by your standards."

"Oh, Chief. You say the sweetest things," I said, laughing. "But him coming down for a visit to see how things are going with his restaurant is the perfect cover. What are they up to now?"

The Chief snuck a glance back. "Let's go with getting friendly and leave it at that," he said, settling back into his seat. "I still can't believe he and your mom used to be an item."

"Based on her mood since they reconnected, I don't think she ever got over him."

"I have a feeling they're about to start making up for lost time," the Chief said. "Tell me again why you're convinced the factory has something to do with the murder."

"Convinced is such a strong word," I said, then waited until he stopped laughing. "But I'm almost positive the company is connected in some way. And since the factory is the only physical location Paddles has, it has to be worth a look, right?"

"Don't ask me," the Chief said. "I'm only here for the margaritas."

"Apart from the factory, that company is pretty much a website and a traveling road show. You know, races and promotional events."

"I still think Charlie might have been killed by somebody else he tried to stiff on a gambling debt," the Chief said.

"Why would Charlie bet with anybody else?" I said. "He had a pretty sweet arrangement worked out with Paulie."

"Maybe it was a bet on something that Paulie doesn't handle," the Chief said. "Some stupid bet Charlie made with another guy. Like who could paddle the fastest to some offshore island. Or maybe a cockfight."

"A cockfight?"

"Yeah, they're pretty popular down there with some folks," the Chief said, shrugging. "And I doubt if Paulie takes action on fighting roosters."

"That's disgusting," I said. "People bet on stuff like that?"

"Sure. And some people bet big on it."

"Barbaric. But I guess it's a possibility," I said, popping another bite-sized. "I still think the company has to be involved somehow."

"But how?" the Chief said. "They make water sports equipment. And they're the fastest growing company in the market."

"I don't know," I said, swallowing. "That's why I want to check out the factory. We'll need to figure out a way to get a tour."

"A tour of what, darling?"

I glanced up at my mother who was standing next to me with Paulie at her side.

"Uh, a tour of Paulie's bungalow," I said, lying through my teeth.

"Uh-huh, of course. Mind if we join you?" she said, sitting down in one of the seats that were facing toward us.

Paulie slid into the seat next to her and beamed at me.

"I need to thank you," he said. "Your mother tells me that this trip was your idea."

"It was," I said, nodding. "I figured I owed both of you. Since I was the reason you two broke up the last time."

"You were only part of the reason, darling."

"Regardless," I said. "I'm just glad you could fit it into your schedule."

"I've wanted to get down there for a while. I haven't been back since we broke ground on the restaurant."

"And that's when you bought your bungalow?"

"It was," Paulie said, then glanced at Chief Abrams. "You look very familiar, Chief."

"We've met."

"Refresh my memory," Paulie said.

"About fifteen years ago," the Chief said. "I was with the state police back then. I interviewed you about a guy we found stuffed in a barrel filled with cement."

"Of course," Paulie said, nodding. "Now I remember. Four Finger Freddie."

"That's the one," the Chief said.

"A tragic event," Paulie said. "At least it was for Freddie. Did you ever happen to catch the people who did it?"

"I don't believe we did," the Chief said.

"The guy only had four fingers?" I said, glancing back and forth at them.

"Yes," the Chief said. "Two on each hand."

"Before or after he ended up in the barrel of cement?"

"Before," the Chief and Paulie said in unison.

"Freddie liked to dabble in woodworking," Paulie said. "Unfortunately, he wasn't very good with a bandsaw."

174

"Or so the story goes," the Chief said, staring at Paulie.

"Urban folklore, Chief," Paulie said, laughing. "But that's all ancient history. Let's talk about Mexico."

"What about it?" the Chief said.

"Well, as much as I'd like to give Suzy credit for her matchmaking abilities, I doubt the two of you are tagging along just to keep an eye on us. We're both a bit old to need chaperones."

I glanced at the Chief who shrugged as if to say, go ahead and tell him.

"We think Paddles, the company that makes the boards and kayaks, is somehow involved in Charlie's murder," I said.

The Chief cleared his throat.

"Well, I'm sure, but the Chief still has his doubts.".

"Your mother mentioned your theory to me," Paulie said. "What's the motive?"

"I'm still working on that," I said, shrugging. "What's your take?"

"My take?" Paulie said, cocking his head. "What makes you think I have an opinion?"

"Nothing," I said. "I'm just curious what your thoughts are. I'm looking for all the help I can get."

"When it comes to motive, they're really aren't that many," Paulie said.

"Money, jealousy, fear, and revenge," I said, rattling them off

"I'm not sure that's all of them, but it's a pretty good list," Paulie said, laughing.

"No, I'm just referring to this case," I said. "Those are the four I've come up with."

"You have been busy, darling."

"Just my usual neuron overload, Mom," I said.

"I'm curious," Paulie said. "Why those four?"

"Well, as soon as I ruled out the idea that…" I paused and gave Paulie a weak grin.

"That I was the one who had him killed?" Paulie said, raising an eyebrow at me. Fortunately, he did it with a big smile.

"Well, yeah," I said, nodding. "As soon as I ruled you out, I decided that it must have had something to do with the company. And since it's a pretty big company, money is always a logical assumption to make."

"It is," Paulie said. "Do you think Charlie was stealing from the company?"

"Well, he didn't work there, so my thinking is, that if he was involved in something like that, he must have had help on the inside."

"That makes sense," Paulie said. "Go on."

"Don't encourage her, Paulie," my mother said, laughing. "Now I see why you two hit it off."

I made a face at my mother then brushed my hair back from my face.

"So, if it did involve money, we might logically assume that someone else who works inside the company might still be in danger," I said, popping another bite-sized.

"Unless they haven't made the connection yet to who might have been working with Charlie," the Chief said.

"Which still leads us to believe that someone else might get killed," I said.

"The easiest way to steal money without anybody finding out is by cooking the books," Paulie said. "Do you know who handles the finances for the company?"

"Yes, her name is Maria, and she's the CEO's girlfriend," I said.

"That's probably worth pursuing," Paulie said.

"That's what I thought at first," I said. "If she was working with Charlie, and Julian, he's the CEO, found out, he could have been the one who organized the hit."

"Organized the hit?" Paulie said, glancing over at my mother. "Does she always talk like this?"

"Don't even get me started," my mother said.

"But then we found Maria's dog in the middle of the River," I said. "And when I talked with Maria after that, she seemed afraid of something. And I mean, she was really scared. I think somebody put her Maltese on that paddleboard and pushed it out into the water just to send her a message. I know it sounds strange, but after I gave it some thought, it made sense to me."

"Any dog lover would completely understand it," Paulie said. "But if anybody ever tried to mess with my dogs, my reaction would be a bit different."

"So would mine," I said. "But if Julian knew that his girlfriend was stealing money from him, why would he even bother sending her a message using the dog? Why wouldn't he just confront her directly?"

"Maybe the CEO doesn't know what's going on," the Chief said.

"I guess Maria could be working with someone else inside the company and has started to feel guilty about it," I said.

"But then you're talking about three people being involved. Maria, Charlie, and this other person," Paulie said.

"And you know what they say about three people being able to keep a secret."

"Yeah, it's possible as long as two of them are dead," I said, nodding at Paulie.

"Okay, that covers money and fear," the Chief said. "What's the possible jealousy angle?"

"That one's a bit of a stretch," I said, offering the bag of bite-sized to everyone. I unwrapped one and popped it into my mouth. "But when I had lunch with all of them, it was pretty clear that Emma, the woman who works for the clothing company, had been involved with Charlie at one point. And I'm positive she's in some sort of relationship with that guy, Matisse, who works for the beer company. I also got a weird vibe from Julian when the conversation turned to who was sleeping with who."

"Whom," the Chief said, grinning at me.

I thought about it, then nodded.

"Well played, Chief," I said, laughing. "I don't have any evidence, but if they're all hooking up with each other, all sorts of people might have been mad enough at Charlie to take him out."

"I don't like it," Paulie said, shaking his head.

"Yeah, like I said, that one is a total stretch. It's really thin."

179

"So, that leaves you with revenge," my mother said.

"That one is a recent addition," I said, glancing at the Chief.

"And not directly connected to Charlie's murder," he said.

"How so?" Paulie said.

"The other kayaker, Gordo, Charlie's best friend, seemed very interested in getting revenge on whoever killed his buddy."

"But that would mean he knows who killed Charlie," Paulie said.

"Or he's traveling to Mexico to see if he can figure it out," I said.

"Just like us," the Chief said.

"Which leads me right back to my idea that the answer lies somewhere in that factory," I said.

"This is so confusing. There are just so many possibilities," my mother said, frowning.

"Now you see why I get all those headaches," I said.

"Don't go for self-pity, darling. It's not becoming."

"Thanks for the reminder, Mom," I said. "All we'll need to do is come with a good excuse for paying them a visit."

"That shouldn't be a problem," Paulie said.

"Why not?"

180

"Because I invited Julian to have dinner at my restaurant tonight," he said, grinning at me. "And I told him to feel free to invite anyone else he wanted to bring along."

"You did what?" my mother said, staring at him.

"I figured the least I could do was to help speed up the process a bit," Paulie said.

"What reason did you use as an excuse to invite them to dinner?" the Chief said.

"I'm thinking about opening a surf shop in the area, and I'm going to need a lot of rental equipment," Paulie said.

"You're planning on opening a surf shop?" I said.

"Of course not," Paulie said. "But they don't know that."

"I knew I liked you for a reason," I said, grinning at him. "Mom, don't ever let him go."

"That's the plan, darling."

I flinched, studied her closely, then realized she wasn't joking. She tucked her head against his shoulder, and they nuzzled and whispered contentedly. I watched them, then looked at the Chief and shrugged.

I guess having one more ex-gangster in the family couldn't hurt.

Chapter 17

We landed in Mazatlán, made our way through immigration without any problems, then headed for the large SUV Paulie had rented. I watched him and my mother closely as they discussed the logistics and was impressed by how comfortable they were with each other. I climbed into the backseat with the Chief, and we headed into the city, then drove north for a few minutes until we reached the small beach town of Punta Chicado. Paulie slowly drove through the center of town, glancing around as if seeing it for the first time, and paying close attention to the various things my mother was pointing out which included his restaurant. A few minutes later, he turned off the road onto a winding, single-lane driveway with high, landscaped foliage on both sides. About a hundred yards later, the driveway ended, and we came to a stop in front of a sprawling single-story structure that fronted the beach.

"This is your *bungalow*?" I said, staring out the window.

"That's what the real estate agent called it," Paulie said, with a shrug as he hopped out of the SUV. "So, I just stuck with it."

I climbed out and took some time to take it all in.

"Well, I guess you don't have to worry about him only being interested in your mom's money," the Chief said, shaking his head in amazement. Then he called out to Paulie. "How many bedrooms does this place have?"

"Nine, I think," Paulie said, starting to unload our luggage. "But I've only been here the one time."

"It's incredible," my mother said.

"Now that you're here, it's incredible," Paulie said, beaming at my mother. "Before that, it was just really nice."

"Aren't you sweet," my mother said, then glanced over her shoulder at me. "Are you taking notes, darling? That is how it's done."

"Got it, Mom," I said, laughing. "C'mon, Chief. Let's go raid the fridge and leave these lovebirds alone."

"You feel like a margarita?"

"I thought you'd never ask," I said, following him toward the house.

We walked around to the front of the house that fronted the beach and climbed the short set of steps that led up to the verandah. I looked out at the ocean and the surf that was rolling in. Several surfers were expertly weaving their way across the water, while others were bodysurfing near shore. Further out to sea past the surf break, I could see a handful of windsurfers speeding along in the stiff breeze.

183

"I'm getting worn out just watching them," I said, eventually.

"Nice life, though," he said, staring out at the ocean. "I can see why they built their factory here."

"But there are hundreds of great surf locations around," I said, still struggling with one of the questions that continued to nag at me. "Why here?"

"Why not?" the Chief said, shrugging.

"Yeah, I guess you're right," I said, looking back out over the water. "Why not indeed?"

We both turned around when Paulie opened the doors from inside the house. He stepped out onto the verandah and took a deep breath.

"Not bad, huh?" he said, staring out at the water. "I thought we'd relax for a few hours then head to the restaurant. I told this guy Julian we'd be there no later than seven.

"That works," I said. "I'm going to make a pitcher of margaritas. Care to join us?"

"No, thanks," he said. "Maybe later. I think your mom and I are going to take a nap. Help yourself to anything you'd like."

He gave us a casual wave then headed back inside.

"A nap?" I said, laughing as I glanced at the Chief. "Is that what we're calling it these days?"

"Hey, maybe they are going to take one," he said, laughing along as he followed me into the house. "It was a long flight."

"Actually, a nap sounds pretty good," I said, heading for the kitchen to find the blender.

My phone rang, and I glanced at the number. Josie. I answered it on the second ring.

"Hey," I said. "Hang on just a sec." I looked at the Chief. "It's Josie. You mind making the drinks?"

"Not a problem," he said, heading for the cupboards. "Tell her I said hi."

I walked back out onto the porch and sat down and put my feet up. I glanced around and got the feeling that I'd forgotten something. Then I realized what the problem was. No dogs.

"How's it going?" I said into the phone.

"It's really quiet," she said. "But I guess that's understandable."

"Funny."

"Chef Claire is taking the night off, and we invited Jackson and Freddie over for dinner."

185

"What are you having?" I said, switching the phone to my other ear.

"I think we're just going to do a fridge clean," she said. "How's Mexico?"

"Well, Paulie's place is right on the water, and it's magnificent," I said, watching a surfer effortlessly work her way across a large wave. "And my mother is officially in love."

"Good for her."

"No, I mean she's a total goner," I said. "I don't think I've ever seen her like this."

"Happy's what we're all going for, right?"

"Absolutely," I said, glancing up as the Chief stepped onto the porch carrying two glasses. I took a sip and gave him a nod of approval. I put the phone on speaker and set it down on the armrest. "Chief says hi."

"Hi, Chief," Josie chirped.

"Hey, Josie. How's it going?"

"Great. It's nice and peaceful around here at the moment."

"Well, that's completely understandable," he said.

He and Josie laughed. I waited it out.

"So, what's your plan?" Josie said.

"We're having dinner with Julian and some of the people from Paddles," I said. "From there, we'll probably just wing it."

"Good call," she deadpanned. "Play to your strengths."

"It was nice talking to you, Josie," I said, shaking my head.

"Hang on. I haven't told you why I called," she said. "Maria called the Inn this afternoon and said she'd be picking up the Maltese the day after tomorrow."

"Did she say where she is at the moment?"

"Mexico."

"Okay, that means she'll probably be at dinner," I said. "I hope we can get what we need down here then head home. I'd like to be there when she picks the dog up."

"That might be a good idea. Because she's not coming by herself," Josie said, her voice rising in a sing-song voice.

"Julian's coming with her?" I said, glancing at the Chief who was listening closely.

"Nope. Do you know some guy named Kirk?"

"Kirk? He's one of the board designers I met at the house. Why is he tagging along?"

"Apparently, they forgot a few things when they left the Anderson place. And they need to swing by to grab them."

"Did she say what they forgot?"

"Nope."

"Okay," I said, not finding the information particularly important or useful.

"But they're going to be picking up whatever it is around eight o'clock the day after tomorrow," Josie said. "Right after sunset. Her words, not mine."

I frowned and looked at the Chief.

"Did you have to ask her what time they were going to pick the stuff up?"

"I did not," Josie said. "She just sort of blurted it out. And it sounded like she was almost asking, without actually coming out and saying it, for somebody to be there waiting when they showed up."

"You mean, somebody like the cops?" I said.

"I'm not sure," she said. "It was a weird conversation. But it definitely came across like it was some sort of cry for help."

"Did it sound like somebody might have been listening to what she was saying on the phone?"

"Nothing gets past you," Josie said, laughing. "That's exactly what it sounded like."

"Interesting."

"You were right, Suzy. That woman is scared to death of something."

188

"But what?" I said, shrugging.

"I have no idea," Josie said. "But I'm sure you'll figure it out. I wish I could be there with you guys. I've been jonesing for Mexican food."

"No, we're having pizza tonight," I said, my neurons firing.

"And I thought driving to Rochester was a long way to go for a pie," she said. "Silly me. Okay, have fun. But be careful and try not to do anything stupid."

"Thanks, Coach. Very inspirational."

"Hey, it's what I do," she said, laughing. "Later."

I slid my phone into my pocket and looked at the Chief.

"What do you think?" I said.

"I have no idea what it means. Or if it means anything at all," he said, taking a sip of his margarita. "But I suppose it couldn't hurt to ask Detective Williams to keep an eye on the place in case we don't make it back in time."

"And tag along if we do, right?" I said.

"Geez, Suzy," the Chief said, frowning. "I just got back in her good graces."

"You don't have to worry about that," I said, shaking my head. "I got a one-year reprieve from the Governor."

"You did?" he said, confused.

"Yeah, it's sort of like a hall pass," I said. "Or maybe it's just a deal with the devil. But I will need to keep my end of the bargain. Hey, you don't happen to know any cute and eligible bachelors, do you?"

Chapter 18

Apart from being a bit smaller than his restaurant in Rochester, Paulie's new place in Punta Chicado was nearly identical in design. As such, I didn't need to ask for directions to the bathroom. As soon as we entered, I headed for the ladies' room in the back of the restaurant with an intense focus on the task at hand and a very full bladder. A few minutes later I exited the bathroom feeling and walking much better. I scanned the restaurant for signs of my mother and ran straight into a man who was heading in the other direction and talking on his phone. I went down hard and bounced a few times on Mexican tile before coming to a stop. I grimaced and rolled over on my back and started to sit up when I noticed an extended hand a few inches away from my face offering assistance.

"You might want to watch where you're…" I snapped, then trailed off.

We'd made eye contact at the exact same moment, and both flinched. I immediately forgot about the possibility of injury and looked up at the man who was staring at me with a concerned look on his face.

191

"I'm so sorry. Are you okay?" he said softly, putting his phone away as he knelt down.

"Who cares?" I said, resting on my elbows as I continued to stare at the stranger.

"What?"

"Forget it," I said, cocking my head. "It's probably just a concussion."

"Oh, let's hope not," he said, extending his hand again.

This time I accepted it, and he gently helped me to my feet. We continued to stare at each other, and I pushed my hair back, rocked back and forth on my heels, and tried to focus on my breathing.

"Again, I'm so sorry," he said. "That's what I get for trying to walk and talk at the same time."

"No, it's my fault," I said, unable to take my eyes off him. "I wasn't paying attention." Then I exhaled loudly. "But I am now." I was about to extend my arm to shake his hand when I realized he was already holding mine. "I'm Suzy."

"It's nice to meet you, Suzy," he said, his eyes boring into me as he continued to hold and gently squeeze my hand. "I'm Max. Max Jenkins."

"Max. Good name," I said. "I think I'm going to need that hand, Max."

"Of course," he said, tightening his grip. "I'm sorry about that. It just feels so good holding it."

I flinched again and swallowed hard.

"Well, it's not like I'm going to need it back right this second."

He laughed and let go. Unsure what to do with his hands, he eventually decided to let them hang by his side, and we continued to stare at each other oblivious to the noise and the other people walking past us.

"This is…awkward," he said, his face turning red.

"That's a word for it," I said softly. "You're Canadian, aren't you?"

"You have a good ear," Max said. "I live in Ottawa, but I grew up in a little town on the St. Lawrence River."

"You're joking, right?"

"I'm not exactly sure what I'm doing at the moment," he said, shaking his head. "But I'm positive I'm not joking. I grew in a place called Gananoque."

"Clay Bay," I said, shrugging.

"Really?" he said, relaxing as he folded his arms across his chest. He beamed at me. "That's amazing. What are you doing here?"

"I'm just down here with my mother and her boyfriend. Actually, this is his restaurant," I said, as casually as I could.

193

"Amazing pizza," Max said, locking eyes with me again.

"That's good to hear," I said, glancing back at the empty booth directly behind me.

I casually reached back with one arm in an attempt to strike a relaxed pose without taking my eyes off him. My hand brushed the back of the booth then slid off, and I lost my balance, stumbled backward, then fell onto the tile floor again.

"Smooth," I whispered, shaking my head at my clumsiness.

"Are you okay?" he said, again helping me to my feet.

"No, actually, I don't think I am," I said, staring at him.

"What's the matter?" he said, concerned.

"Who are you?" I whispered. "And where did you come from?"

"I beg your pardon?"

"I mean, why are you here in Punta Chicado?"

"We just decided to come here for a couple of days to do some surfing before we headed home," he said, shrugging.

"I knew there had to be a catch," I said, shaking my head.

"What?"

"The dreaded we," I said, shrugging.

"Oh, that," Max said, laughing. "No, I was referring to one of my co-workers. He's a big-time surfer, and I decided to tag along. And I have to say that I'm very glad I did."

"Not half as glad as I am," I whispered as I grabbed a napkin off one of the tables and brushed myself off.

"What? I'm sorry I didn't hear you."

"Lucky for me," I said, flashing him a quick smile. "What do you do?"

"I'm a disaster relief consultant," he said. "I've been down here helping out with some of the earthquake recovery efforts."

"You could have given me a thousand guesses, and I wouldn't have gotten that," I said, finally locating the back of the booth with my hand. I leaned against it and did my best to look relaxed and cool.

"What would your first guess have been?" he said, now completely at ease.

"I don't know," I said, shrugging. "Neuron Accelerator?"

"I have no idea what you're talking about," he said, laughing.

"Yeah, I really need to start working on that."

"I'm sorry to run you over then leave," he said, glancing down at his watch. "But I'm running very late."

"For what?" I said, crushed.

"I need to get to the airport. My flight home leaves in about an hour and a half."

"You could always run away from home," I said, cocking my head and grinning at him.

"Tempting," he said. "Very tempting indeed."

He removed a business card from his wallet and handed it to me. I glanced down at it then slid it into my pocket. Then he handed me a second card.

"Don't worry," I said. "I won't lose it."

"No, I need your number," he said, handing me a pen. "Just jot it down on the back of the card. Please."

I did, checked to make sure it was legible then handed the card back to him. He slid it into his wallet then gently grabbed my hand.

"I almost skipped dinner," he said, squeezing my hand. "That could have been one of the biggest mistakes I've ever made."

"Sure, you gotta eat, right?"

"When are you heading home?" he said.

"A couple of days," I said, patting the outside of my pocket to make sure his card was still there. "You'll call me?"

"I certainly will," he said, letting go of my hand. "And if drive down, maybe we can grab some dinner?"

"I could eat," I said, nodding.

"I've got a strange feeling," he said.

"Oh, good, you feel it, too," I said, laughing. "I'd hate to think it was just me."

"No, it's definitely not just you," Max said. "I'll call you. Soon."

He reached out and gently stroked the side of my face with the back of his hand. He was lucky we were in a crowded restaurant because, if we weren't, he never would have made his flight. I watched him exit through a side door, then made my way back into the dining area. I spotted my mother at a table set for twelve laughing and chatting with Paulie and the Chief. She spotted me making my way through the tables and waved. I sat down next to her, my neurons still flaring.

"I thought you might have gotten lost, darling. Are you okay?"

"I'm fine," I said, staring off into the distance.

"You look like you've seen a ghost," she said, studying my face closely.

"No, he wasn't a ghost," I said.

"He?"

"Yeah," I said, reaching into my pocket and handing her the business card.

"Max Jenkins," she said, reading from it. "Disaster Relief Consultant? From Ottawa. Interesting." She looked back at me. "Did you just get your bell rung, darling?"

"I think it's still ringing," I said, glancing over at her. "That's never happened to me before. At least like that."

"I know exactly what you're talking about," she said, nodding.

"Really?"

"Yes, it's happened to me twice."

"Dad?"

"Yes, of course," she said, patting Paulie's hand. "And this guy here was the second."

"I guess that explains why you guys reconnected so quickly," I said.

"Yes, I'm sure it does," she said.

"I'm really happy for you, Mom."

"Thank you. And I'm happy for you, darling. Delighted, actually."

"Don't get too far ahead of yourself, Mom. I just met the guy."

"But you're interested in him, right?"

"I certainly am."

"Well, there you go," she said, laughing. "Problem solved."

"I'm not following."

"It's just that I know what a tenacious little monster you can be when you get fixated on something."

"Monster is a bit strong, wouldn't you say?"

"I guess we'll see how it plays out, won't we?"

I laughed and shook my head. I accepted the glass of beer Paulie had poured for me and all four of us clinked glasses. Then my neurons focused on the task at hand.

"But speaking of tenacious, what's keeping our dinner guests?" I said, glancing around the restaurant.

Chapter 19

Our guests did arrive a few minutes later, and the hostess escorted the group of eight led by a smiling Julian to the table. I had to glance over my shoulder to get a good look at them, and realized it was the same people that had stayed at the Anderson house during the 147. Maria was the first to spot me, and she waved and made her way to my end of the table and sat down next to me.

"Suzy," she said, obviously surprised. "What on earth are you doing here?"

"Just tagging along with my mom and her boyfriend," I said. "I've never been here before and a couple days in the sun sounded good."

"Do you always go on vacation with the chief of police?" she said, giving me a coy smile.

"The Chief is like a member of the family," I said. "And he's one of my fishing buddies. I promised we'd spend at least one day trying to catch a sailfish or a marlin."

"That sounds like fun," she said, smiling as she waved at the Chief and my mother. "How's Mellow doing?"

"She's great," I said. "Josie called earlier and said you were going to pick her up the day after tomorrow."

"I am," she said, then frowned briefly before glancing down the table. "Hey, guys. Look who's here."

I leaned forward and waved to everyone who returned my hello. I watched the Chief slide down one seat to give Julian the chance to sit next to Paulie. The CEO smiled at my mother and me, then he focused on Paulie.

"Thanks for the invitation, Mr. Provincial," Julian said. "We eat here all the time when we're in town. I had no idea who owned the place. So, you're a restaurant guy, huh?"

"I am," Paulie said, nodding. "But the town looks like it could use another surf shop, so I thought I might give it a shot. And please call me Paulie."

"Paulie it is," Julian said, nodding. "So, you'll need inventory to open the shop. We can certainly help you with that."

I leaned over and whispered to my mother. "The Chief and I are going to head out soon."

"What?" my mother said, turning away from the conversation Paulie and Julian were having to focus on me. "Where are you going?"

"Nowhere in particular," I said, lying through my teeth. "But I might stick around long enough to have a couple of slices."

My mother gave me a blank stare.

"Hey, we made a deal, Mom. Let it go."

"All right, darling," she said, then focused on Paulie who was talking to her. She glanced back at me briefly. "I just hope I brought enough money for bail."

"Funny."

"I love the pizza here," Maria said to me after waving off the server's offer of a menu. "I have no idea why the owner decided to open a place here, but I'm sure glad he did."

I'd been wondering if she had known that the original suggestion to open the restaurant had come from Charlie, but based on the way she tossed the comment out, I was pretty sure she would have been surprised to hear that bit of news. But there was no reason to raise her suspicions by revealing that Paulie had been Charlie's bookie. I kept sneaking glances at the Chief until I made eye contact with him, and nodded my head toward the door. He frowned and shook his head. I made a second attempt to get him to follow my lead. Again, he refused with a shake of his head.

"Man, I'm starving," he said to no one in particular, ignoring me completely.

Then the Chief flashed me a grin. I made a face at him then glanced around the table. Rock and Kirk, the two board designers, were in the middle of a quiet but intense conversation. Emma and Matisse were sitting across the table from each other and sneaking the occasional knowing glance. Why the two sponsors were in Mexico was a mystery. But I didn't give it a lot of thought since both their companies were actively engaged with Paddles. Layla and Kim, the two sales reps, were sitting next to each other at the far end of the table chatting and laughing.

Our server arrived with salads, and I began working on mine as I continued to make small talk with Maria. They were here for their monthly meeting, Emma and Matisse were in town to discuss some contractual issues, and Paddles was getting ready to roll out their latest board designs that had the potential to revolutionize the industry. As soon as Maria started prattling on about aerodynamics and tensile strength, my neurons decided it was time for a nap, and I began glancing around the dining room for signs of our pizzas. Three large pies were soon delivered steaming hot, and I dug right in and burned my mouth three times before I finally learned my lesson.

I was hungry, but the primary reason I was forcing the scalding hot pizza down was that I wanted to hit the road while everyone was still eating dinner. Three quick slices later, I wiped my mouth with a napkin and made eye contact with the Chief again. I caught him mid-bite, and he finished chewing before finally nodding. I took my cue and grabbed my phone from my pocket. I glanced down at the screen, then put the phone away.

"Hey, Chief," I said, loud enough for others to hear. "I just got a text from the guy we're renting the boat from tomorrow. He's got a couple questions for us."

"About what?" the Chief said, giving me a small smile.

I glared at him. I hadn't expected to have to go into any details with my cover story. But two could play that game.

"He said he had a problem processing your credit card payment," I said, giving him a crocodile grin. "Are you sure you paid your bill?"

"I'm sure it's just a mistake," the Chief said, giving up and sliding his chair back.

"He also said he wants to go over a few things with us for tomorrow," I said, getting up out of my seat. "Mom, the Chief and I need to go have a chat with the boat captain. We'll just meet you back at the house later."

"Okay, darling," she said, giving me her best *stay out of trouble* look.

"Thanks for dinner, Paulie," I said, then glanced around the table. "It was great seeing all of you."

The rest of the group glanced up long enough to wave goodbye then went back to their conversations.

204

"Will you be back home by the time I drop by to pick up Mellow?" Maria said.

"Oh, I'll be there," I said, patting her shoulder on my way past. "I wouldn't miss it for the world."

I led the way toward the front door and held it open for the Chief as he walked outside carrying a slice he'd grabbed before he left the table. I joined him at the bottom of the steps and looked around. My neurons flared and landed on a question.

"Uh-oh," I said.

"Oh, what's the matter? Did you forget something?" the Chief deadpanned.

"You know I did," I said, annoyed. "Why didn't you say something earlier?"

"Because I didn't want to miss the look on your face," he said, laughing.

"How the heck are we going to get there?"

"It looks like we're going to have to walk," he said, extending his arms and bending slightly to take a bite without spilling sauce all over himself.

"Walk? Geez," I said, taking another look around. "I can't believe I forgot about that. A taxi is out of the question, right?"

"I'm not sure this place has taxis," the Chief said. "But even if they do, we can't take the risk of leaving a trail like that."

"No, we can't," I said. "And we can't borrow Paulie's rental, either."

"Nope."

"So we have to hoof it."

"Yup."

"How far do you think it is from here?" I said, staring into the distance at the Paddles' sign that sat on top of the factory on the edge of town.

"It can't be more than a mile," the Chief said. "Let's go."

He tossed back the final remnants of his slice and started walking at a brisk pace. I did my best to keep up with him, but five minutes later, I was huffing and puffing, and the pizza I'd gulped down was sitting like a lump in my stomach.

"How you doing back there?" the Chief said, laughing as he glanced over his shoulder.

"I've been better," I snapped.

"Let me know if there are any other details you forgot to work out," he said. "I'll see what I can do to help you out."

"You're really not funny, Chief."

By the time we reached the outer edge of the parking lot that fronted the factory, I was doubled over, my legs were on fire, and I would have killed for a couple hits from an oxygen tank. The Chief waited patiently for me to catch my breath, and I eventually stood upright and put my hands on my hips.

"What's next, Snoopmeister?"

"I have no idea."

"That's quite a plan you've put together there, Suzy," he deadpanned as he looked around. "No moon. That's going to make it a bit harder to see what we're doing."

"Now that is something I do have covered," I said, reaching into my bag and removing a pair of night-vision binoculars.

"You brought those with you?" the Chief said.

"You sound surprised," I said, looking through the binoculars and scanning the empty parking lot and dark factory.

"Let me take a look," he said, holding out a hand.

I handed him the glasses and waited until he finished surveilling the immediate area. Then he handed them back to me.

"We need to get inside," I said.

"You want to break in? Have you ever heard the rumors about what it's like being in a Mexican prison?"

"Yes, I have," I said, taking another look through the glasses.

"Well, just for the sake of argument, let's assume they're all true."

"Don't worry, Chief. We're not going to prison."

"Yeah, you're probably right," he said. "I'm sure we'll just be shot on sight."

"You worry way too much," I said, catching a glimpse of movement. "Hang on. I think I see somebody."

I handed him the binoculars and pointed at the right side of the building.

"Got him," the Chief said. "It looks like he's trying to get that door open."

"Is he using a key?" I said, reaching for the glasses.

"Well, it's a little hard to tell when you're constantly grabbing the binoculars," the Chief said, annoyed.

"You should have remembered to bring your own. No, he definitely doesn't have a key," I said, staring intensely at what the man was doing. "He's picking the lock. And now he's in."

I lowered the glasses and looked at the Chief. He stared back at me then shrugged.

"Okay, I guess we've come this far," he said.

We left the sandy trail and stepped onto the paved parking lot and headed for the factory, hugging the side of the building as we made our way down to the door that was ajar.

"Are you ready?" I said, reaching for the door handle.

"Let me go first," he whispered. "Give me the glasses and hold onto the back of my shirt so I don't lose you."

Moments later, we were inside the dark factory, and I felt myself being pulled to the right. We came to a stop, and the Chief patted my hand. I took it as a mandate to remain quiet. He slowly continued working his way along the wall then came to a sudden stop. I bumped up against him, and he stumbled slightly then stepped on my foot.

"Ow," I whispered. "Watch where you're going."

"Shhh," the Chief said. "We need to get behind that stack of surfboards off to our left."

"I'll take your word for it," I whispered in the darkness.

I shuffled my feet as I followed the Chief then felt the presence of the surfboards directly in front of me.

"What's he doing?" I whispered.

"He's just looking around at the moment," he said.

"Can you see his face?"

"No, he's still got his back to us. Hang on. He's reaching into his pocket."

"Gun?"

A beam of light appeared on the other side of the factory floor.

"Flashlight," the Chief whispered.

"Yeah, thanks for clearing that up," I said, shaking my head.

"Shhh. He's reaching for something else."

"Gun, right?"

"I don't believe it," the Chief said.

"What is it?"

"It's a bag of bite-sized. Are you freaking kidding me?"

"Well, the guy certainly knows his candy. You gotta give him that," I said, reaching for the binoculars. The Chief reluctantly handed them over, and I focused them on the man who still had his back to us. "He's got the flashlight focused on a set of double doors."

"Is he trying to pick the lock?" the Chief whispered.

"No, it's got one of those keypads you punch your password into," I said. "But he's obviously very interested in what's behind those doors. Hang on, he's turning around. Well, what do you know?"

"It's Gordo, isn't it?"

"Well done, Chief," I said, glancing over at him. "How the heck did you know that?"

210

"Lucky guess," he whispered.

"Uh-oh," I said.

"What's the matter?"

"He's heading straight toward us," I said, staring through the binoculars and scanning our immediate area for a better place to hide. "Better get your cover story ready. We're about to get busted."

Then the Chief's booming voice reverberated around the factory.

"Baile justo allí. Ponga sus manos en sus tobillos y saltar alrededor!"

Gordo came to an immediate stop and glanced around with a very confused look on his face.

"Ponga sus manos en sus tobillos y saltar alrededor!" the Chief repeated.

Despite the situation we found ourselves in, I bit my hand hard to stop myself from laughing.

"What's the matter?" the Chief said, grabbing the binoculars from me. "What the heck is he doing?"

"I think your Spanish needs a bit of work, Chief," I whispered.

"My Spanish is just fine," he whispered in return. Then he called out again. "Baile justo allí!" Then he fell silent. I assumed the Chief was studying Gordo's reaction through the binoculars. "What the heck is the matter with him?"

"This I gotta see," I said, taking the binoculars back and watching the man trying to assume what looked like a bad yoga pose. I stifled a loud snort. "I cannot wait to tell this story."

Gordo slowly stood, frantically glanced around for any sign of the man behind the voice, then pointed the beam at the door. He switched the flashlight off, and I watched him make a beeline for the exit. Moments later, he was out the door, and I heard the sound of footsteps running across the parking lot. I might have tried to follow him if I hadn't been doubled over in laughter.

"What on earth was that all about?" the Chief said.

"Baile justo allí? Ponga sus manos en sus tobillos y saltar alrededor?" I said, tears rolling down my cheek.

"Yeah. I said: Halt right there. Put your hands in the air and don't move," the Chief said, baffled. "What the heck was wrong with that?"

"Actually, what you said was: Dance right there. Put your hands on your ankles and jump around."

"I did?"

"Yeah."

"Well, that explains his confusion," the Chief said, heading for the door that was partially open.

I heard the door close, and we were again standing in total darkness.

"Help me find my way back," he said.

I walked to the door, grabbed his hand and led him to the center of the factory floor. I glanced around through the binoculars.

"What do you think about turning the lights on?" I said.

"Not a good idea," he said. "If they have surveillance cameras installed, we'd be totally busted."

"Unless they have night-vision surveillance installed," I said, shrugging. "If they do, they've already got us on camera."

"I'll take my chances," the Chief said. "But no lights."

"Yeah, you're probably right," I said, turning my head toward the locked doors Gordo had been interested in. "I sure would like to get a look at what's behind those doors."

"Shhh," the Chief said. "I hear somebody."

"You think he grabbed a gun and decided to come back?" I said, leading him toward the stack of surfboards we'd been hiding behind earlier.

"Why are you fixated on guns all of a sudden?" he said.

"Well, I did get shot the last time we did this."

"What happened to *it was just a flare gun?*"

"That was just to get my mother off my back. But he ran out of here in a panic. He wouldn't come back, would he?"

"Anything's possible," the Chief said.

"He probably gave it some thought and decided that no cop would ever tell him to grab his ankles and jump around," I said, stifling a laugh.

"Just let it go, okay?" the Chief whispered.

"Oh, I don't like your chances, Chief."

"Shhh."

I crouched down behind the surfboards and peered through the binoculars.

"What the heck? The door is unlocked. How many times have I told you to make sure the place is locked up tight before you leave?"

"I did, Rock," the board designer named Kirk said. "I checked it twice."

"Then it appears we might have a visitor," Rock said softly as he slowly stepped inside.

Through the binoculars, I watched both men slowly reach behind their backs and pull handguns out. Then we both heard the unmistakable sound of a shell being racked into the chamber of both guns.

"My mother is going to kill me," I whispered.

"Don't...do a...thing," the Chief whispered, squeezing my arm hard to emphasize his point.

Then the factory floor was bathed in light. We crouched even lower as we watched both men slowly sweep the area with intense stares, their guns extended.

"Okay," Rock said softly. "If there is somebody here, we know what they're looking for. C'mon, follow me."

They both slowly worked their way across the floor until they reached the double doors on the other side of the room. I trained the binoculars on the keypad and focused hard as I watched Rock enter the password. The lock clicked open, and they stepped inside closing the door behind them.

"Okay, let's get out of here," the Chief said, pulling my arm as he raced for the door.

I followed him muttering to myself. We stepped outside, and I did my best lumber across the parking lot.

"7,2,3,3,5,3,7.   7,2,3,3,5,3,7.   7,2,3,3,5,3,7," I kept repeating. "Write that down before I forget it."

"What is it?" the Chief said, frowning as he reached for his notepad.

"It's the password Rock just entered," I said. "7,2,3,3,5,3,7."

"Got it," he said, scribbling the number sequence down. "Let's go."

"Where are we going?"

"Well, I don't know about you," he said, exiting the parking lot and hopping onto the sandy trail that led back to the main street of town. "But I thought I might head back to Paulie's place. It's been a very long day."

"Okay," I said, following him. "How far do you think it is?"

"It can't be more than a couple of miles. Piece of cake."

"That's easy for you to say," I said, my breathing already starting to become labored. "Man, this really sucks."

"Suzy?"

"Yeah."

"Please, stop whining."

"It was just an observation," I said, coming to a stop to deal with a stitch in my side. "But I suppose it could be worse."

"How's that?"

"I could be holding onto my ankles and trying to jump around," I said, laughing as I resumed walking.

"You're really not as funny as you think you are."

"Voy a tener que estar en desacuerdo contigo, mi buen amigo."

"What?" the Chief said, glancing back over at his shoulder with a deep frown etched on his face.

"Look it up."

Chapter 20

From the comfort of my recliner, I held out my glass, and Chief poured a fresh margarita from the pitcher he was holding. I glanced up at him, my phone still tucked against my ear.

"Thanks, Chief."

He stretched out on the recliner next to mine, and I put the phone on speaker and set it down on the small table between the lounge chairs. The sound of Josie's laughter reverberated around the verandah.

"Ponga sus manos en sus tobillos y saltar alrededor?" she said through the phone as soon as she got her laughter under control. "Pretty smooth, Chief."

"Hey, I took Spanish way back in high school," he said, defending himself. "I'm lucky I remembered that much."

"It sounds like a command the cop from the Village People would use," Josie said.

"Regardless," the Chief snapped. "It worked."

"So, Snoopmeister," Josie said. "You got a plan for how you want to handle Maria when she stops by to pick up Mellow?"

"Absolutely."

The Chief snorted, and I shot him a dirty look he ignored. He took a sip of his margarita and stared out at the ocean with a big grin.

"Good, I'm glad to hear that," Josie said. "Now, tell me all about this guy you met."

"Let's save that until I get back," I said, stifling a yawn. "I'm still trying to process it. And I doubt these margaritas are going to help clarify my thinking."

"Okay, then I'm going to head back to the living room," Josie said. "Chef Claire and I are trying to watch a movie, but it's a bit hard with seven dogs vying for attention."

"Yeah, I've been meaning to say something about that," I said, frowning. "I think we're going to have to do something with the Labs. Seven dogs are just too many to have in the house. Even for us."

"I agree. But we could always keep them and give them their own condos," Josie said. "That's not a bad life."

"No, it's not. But I think they deserve some acreage," I said. "And if we find a good home, keeping them would just be selfish on our part."

"Whatever's best for the dogs, right?"

"Exactly."

"You got anybody in mind?" Josie said.

"As a matter of fact, I do," I said, glancing up when I heard my mother and Paulie coming out onto the porch. "I'll talk to you tomorrow."

"Later," Josie said. "Hey, Chief?"

"Yeah?"

"Duerme bien, mi amigo desafiado por el español."

"Whatever," the Chief said, scowling at my phone.

Josie and I both laughed, and I ended the call.

"How's Josie doing?" my mother said.

"She's good," I said. "What are you guys doing up?"

"We thought we'd join you for a nightcap," Paulie said, extending two glasses.

The Chief poured from the pitcher, and Paulie stretched out on a recliner. My mother waited until he got settled then slid into the chair with her back against his chest. She wiggled her toes and took a sip, then stared out at the ocean.

"I could get used to this," she said.

"Well, I would certainly hope so," Paulie said, giving her a hug. "So, what did the two of you find out tonight?"

"There's definitely something inside that factory that at least one person wants to get his hands on," the Chief said.

"Did you see who it was?" Paulie said.

"Yeah, it was the guy named Gordo," the Chief said.

"The guy who won the 147?" my mother said, frowning.

"That's the one," I said.

"That's odd," my mother said.

"Did you get a chance to talk to him?" Paulie said.

"No, he disappeared before we had a chance," the Chief said. "I imagine he made his way back to where he's staying."

"Or to a dance club," I deadpanned.

The Chief shot me a dirty look then took another sip.

"What do you think he was looking for?" Paulie said.

"Our best guess at the moment is that he's trying to get his hands on the new board designs Paddles is about to introduce," the Chief said.

"I don't know, Chief," I said. "It's the only thing we've been able to come up with so far, but it seems thin."

"But Maria said they had the potential to revolutionize the industry, right?" the Chief said.

"Yes, she did," I said, taking a sip. I glanced over at Paulie. "What do you think?"

"Do I think that those designs would be enough of a motive to kill somebody over?"

"Yeah."

"I guess if the designs are that good, anything is possible," Paulie said, shrugging. "A little industrial espionage? Yeah, I can see that."

"Those designs would be worth a lot of money to the right person," the Chief said.

"That would mean that Charlie and Gordo were working together trying to steal them?" my mother said.

"It probably would," the Chief said, topping off his glass. "Maybe they thought they could get a better endorsement deal from somebody else. And they wanted to use those designs to sweeten the deal."

"I guess," I said softly. "But why just shoot the one guy? The shooter had the perfect chance to take them both out."

"Yes, he did," the Chief said, shrugging. "Maybe Gordo is working a different angle. Or with different people."

"Maybe. But how do we explain the fact that Maria is definitely scared about something? She's putting up a good front, but something has her very worried. And don't forget that somebody put her Maltese on a paddleboard and floated it out onto the River."

"You don't think that could have just been an accident?"

"No, I don't think it was, Mom. It had to be some sort of warning."

"A warning about what?"

"My guess is to keep her mouth shut," I said. "I don't know. The whole thing is goofy. But now that we've got the password to get into that restricted area in the factory, we should be able to put it together."

"What did you say?" my mother said, sitting up.

"Oh, yeah, I forgot to mention that, didn't I?" I said. "Sorry about that."

"How on earth did you get the password?" Paulie said.

"Night vision binoculars," I said with a shrug.

My mother rubbed her forehead then settled back against Paulie's chest.

"You brought your binoculars with you?" she said.

"Yeah."

"Can I ask why?"

"Because I thought they might come in handy," I said, glancing over at her.

Paulie laughed.

"Please, don't encourage her," my mother said.

I felt the onset of a headache as my neurons surged and then exploded. I closed my eyes as they bounced around inside my head. Then they coalesced on a specific thought, and I grimaced and gripped both armrests with both hands. I grabbed a bottle of Ibuprofen from my bag and washed a small handful down with a sip of my drink. I could have been wrong about the margaritas; maybe they were helping to clarify my thinking.

"Paulie?" I said, sitting up.

"Yeah?"

"Can I ask you a question?"

"Sure, go ahead."

"It's probably going to annoy you," I said, glancing over.

"I think I can handle it," he said.

"Okay, but don't say I didn't warn you," I said, still grimacing from my headache. "Back in the day when you were still dabbling on the dark side, you used your restaurants as a front to cover your tracks, didn't you?"

"Darling! Must you?"

"Wow," Paulie said, laughing. "You were right. That's a very annoying question." He glanced at the Chief. "Given Chief Abrams presence, I'm sure you can understand why I might refrain from answering it."

"Sure, sure," I said. "But speaking hypothetically, it's not unusual for people who might want to stay below the radar to do something like that, right?"

"Speaking hypothetically," he said, smiling at the Chief. "No, that wouldn't be unusual at all."

"What on earth are you talking about, darling?"

"I'm just sitting here thinking about surf shops."

"Man, you could have given me a hundred guesses, and I wouldn't have come up with that," the Chief said, shaking his head.

"You and me both," my mother said, frowning and pointing at my Margarita. "How many of those have you had?"

"I'm fine, Mom," I said. "But a surf shop would be the perfect place to do some interesting things out of."

"If you call selling paddleboards and kayaks interesting, sure," the Chief said.

"What else would a surf shop sell besides boards?" I said, my neurons on fire.

"Well, I imagine they'd sell stuff like snorkeling equipment, swimsuits and beachwear, and probably a bunch of other stuff surfers and tourists would use," the Chief said. "Hats and sunscreen. And tee shirts with catchy slogans."

"Yes, they would, wouldn't they?" I said, settling back into the recliner. I drifted off and looked out at the horizon with an unfocused stare.

"Uh-oh," the Chief said.

"What is it?" Paulie said.

"She's a goner," the Chief said.

"Here we go again," my mother said, shaking her head at me.

"What's the matter with her?" Paulie said, concerned.

"She's fine," my mother said. "Just give her a minute."

"She looks like she just slipped into a coma," Paulie said.

"We should be so lucky," the Chief deadpanned.

"Shut it," I said, maintaining my distant stare.

"Darling?"

"Yes, Mom?"

"Are you all right?"

"I'm fine," I said, returning to my immediate surroundings. "Chief?"

"Yeah?"

"Would you mind giving Detective Williams a call?"

"I can do that," the Chief said. "Now?"

"No, it can wait until the morning," I said, getting up out of the recliner. "I think I'll go to bed."

"Hang on, darling. What's our plan for tomorrow?" my mother said. "Paulie and I were thinking about taking a boat out."

"That sounds nice, Mom," I said, pausing in the doorway. "But I think I'm going to head home."

"What?" the Chief said. "What about our fishing trip?"

"I'll take you out in a couple of days after we get home. We'll see if we can catch a Muskie," I said, starting to drift off again.

"You're going home?" my mother said.

"Yeah, but you guys feel free to stick around," I said. "I'll fly back commercial."

"No, darling," my mother said, glancing at Paulie. "I think I'd rather keep a close eye on you. We'll all go back together. Is that okay with you, Paulie?"

"Sure, it's fine," Paulie said, staring at me. "Are you sure you're okay? You're kinda freaking me out."

"No, really. I'm fine," I said, then glanced around. "What's the name of the state Mazatlán is in?"

"What?" the Chief said, baffled.

"What state are we in at the moment?"

"I'm gonna go with the state of confusion," he said.

"Funny. What's the name of the state?"

"Sinaloa," the Chief said.

"Yeah," I said. "That's what I thought. Good night."

I headed inside, took a quick shower, then stretched out in bed and slept like a baby.

But in the interest of full disclosure, I'm pretty sure the margaritas helped.

Chapter 21

I was quiet on the flight home, and the others eventually gave up trying to engage me in small talk and spent most of their time playing three handed cribbage. Josie met the plane when we landed at the small airstrip just outside of Clay Bay, and the Chief and I headed for her car lugging our overnight bags. I paused when I noticed my mother standing at the bottom of the steps extending from the plane laughing and chatting with Paulie. Then she strolled toward the car.

"Slight change of plans, darling."

"What's up?" I said, tossing my bag into the backseat.

"Since Paulie and I were already planning on being away, we thought we'd just keep the plane for another couple of days and take a trip."

"What happened to your wanting to keep an eye on me?" I said, grinning at her.

"Well, you're back home safe and sound now," she said, toeing the grass with the tip of her shoe. "And I'm sure Josie and the Chief can handle it from here." She glanced into the backseat at Chief Abrams. "Isn't that right, Chief?"

"Absolutely," he said, nodding.

"Where are you guys going?" I said.

"Vegas."

"Don't tell me you guys are going to elope."

"Are you out of your freaking mind?" my mother said, giving me her best *are you out of your freaking mind* look.

It was a deadly one-two combination.

"Rhetorical, right?" I said with a grin.

"We're going to gamble, eat, and catch a couple of shows," she said.

"If you make it out of your room," I said, laughing.

"You know me so well, darling," she said, patting my cheek. "Please try to stay out of trouble."

"Will do. Have fun, Mom."

We exchanged waves, and I hopped into the passenger seat.

"Thanks for picking us up," I said to Josie as she headed for the highway.

"No problem. You want to head straight home?"

"I certainly do."

"That's good because there are several dogs who are dying to say hello," Josie said, accelerating. "Did you guys have a good trip?"

"Most useful," I said, nodding. I glanced over my shoulder at the Chief. "What did Detective Williams have to say?"

"He's going to see what he can find out," the Chief said.

"What does he think of my theory?"

"Actually, he was pretty impressed with it," the Chief said. "And so am I. Where did that one come from?"

"I have no idea," I said, shaking my head.

It was true. I didn't have a clue. Maybe I'd just gotten lucky. Maybe the ocean air had cleared my thinking. Maybe three margaritas were the magic number to get my neurons on the same page. Or I suppose I could be completely wrong and about to embarrass myself and become a laughingstock.

But I doubted it. I was convinced I was onto something.

"Are you going to share this theory with me?" Josie said, glancing over at me as put her turn signal on.

"I thought we'd go through it over lunch," I said. "I'm starving."

"That's good because Chef Claire is making ziti," Josie said, turning onto the side road that ran along the edge of the River and eventually led to the Inn. "And she made a lot of it."

"The one with meatballs or the one with sausage?"

"The one with both," Josie said. "She wanted to do something special for you."

"I should leave town more often," I said.

"No argument there."

I made a face at her and felt my stomach rumble.

"So, Chef Claire made ziti?" the Chief said, doing his best to sound casual.

"She did. Would you like to join us for lunch, Chief?" Josie said, grinning at him through the rear-view mirror.

"Well, I'd hate to impose. But I do have a few loose ends to tie up with the Snoopmeister about our plan for tomorrow," he said. "So, I suppose I could make time."

I glanced over at Josie.

"He thinks he can make the time," I said.

"Yeah, I heard," she said, smiling as she looked into the rear-view mirror. "I'm shocked."

I laughed and turned around in my seat.

"We're glad you can join us, Chief."

"Thanks for the invite. What kind of sausage is she using in the ziti?"

"I'm not sure," Josie said. "Does it matter?"

"Absolutely not. I was just wondering."

"It is a good question," Josie said, glancing over at me.

"Well, he is a cop. He's supposed to ask good questions."

"But just not in Spanish," Josie said, glancing over. "I'm glad you're home."

"Me too."

Chapter 22

I was stretched out on the couch in my office with the snoring Chloe draped across my legs. She hadn't left my side since I'd gotten home, and for the past twenty-four hours I'd again experienced and felt the full force of the power of unconditional love. I gently stroked her fur as I stared up at the ceiling and reviewed my plan. As far as plans go, the word that might be used to describe it would be sketchy. But since efforts like this are more art form than science, and all great artists rely on inspiration and improvisation to some degree, I decided that something would come to me if I soon found myself needing help.

I closed my eyes and was about to drift off when the door opened, and Josie strolled in and sat down behind my desk and put her feet up. She removed an open bag of bite-sized from one of the drawers, frowned, then held it up and examined it in the light.

"You been stress eating?" she said, reaching for the remaining small handful.

"They help me think."

"You must have a lot on your mind," she said, crumpling the empty bag and tossing it into the trash.

"Funny."

"I thought so," she said, flashing me a quick smile. "Okay, you dodged the question all last night. It's time to spill the beans about this guy you met."

"There's really not much to say," I said, sitting up on the couch. Chloe stirred and rearranged herself on my lap. "We literally bumped into each other at the restaurant and only talked for a few minutes."

"But he rang your bell," Josie said, popping a bite-sized.

"Totally," I said. "It was a weird feeling. I've never experienced anything quite like that before. Have you?"

"Twice," Josie said. "Once when I was college, but that turned out to be just an infatuation. And the other was…well, you know who the other one was."

"Summerman."

"Yeah."

Summerman was Josie's on and off boyfriend who was only around during the summer months. But this year, summer had come and gone with no trace of him. At first, Josie, along with the rest of us, had worried that something had happened to him. Her worry soon turned to anger. Then as the weeks passed, he became less of a topic of conversation, and all questions about his whereabouts eventually disappeared altogether. And as the summer progressed, Josie had made it abundantly clear that she didn't want to talk about it, so I let it go.

"Max is probably just an infatuation," I said, shrugging.

"Maybe. But there's only one way to find out," Josie said, rummaging through another desk drawer. She pulled out a fresh bag of bite-sized and ripped it open.

"I didn't know there was another bag in there," I said.

"I know you didn't," she said, grabbing a handful. "Hence, it was still there."

"Where's the trust?" I said, laughing.

"So, what does this guy look like?"

"That's the weird part," I said, gently sliding Chloe off my lap so I could tuck my legs underneath me. "He's cute, but there's really nothing remarkable about the way he looks."

"Then you are in big trouble, my friend."

"Yeah, I know. If he was gorgeous, I could probably just chalk it up to that infatuation thing."

"Uh-huh. He's a disaster relief consultant?"

"That's what he and his business card say."

"He goes to places that have been hit by things like an earthquake or hurricane and comes up with strategies to help the people out?"

"Yeah," I said, nodding.

234

"Strike two," Josie said, laughing. "What he does for a living really got your attention, didn't it?"

"It sure did. What we try to do for dogs, he does for people. What's not to like about that?"

"Not a thing. And he grew up across the River in Gananoque. That's weird. Small world, huh?"

"And he lives in Ottawa when he's not off trying to save it," I said.

"I think you should invite him down here to spend a weekend," Josie said, popping another bite-sized.

"Just so you and Chef Claire can check him out?" I said, raising an eyebrow.

"Nothing gets past you," she said, grinning. "You do want our opinion, don't you?"

"Of course, I do," I said, exhaling audibly. "I'm just nervous about the whole thing."

"That it's going to blow up in your face or that it turns out to be the best thing that ever happened to you?"

"Yup."

"You're worried about both possibilities?" Josie said, studying me closely.

"I am."

"Strike three."

"I know. And I never got the bat off my shoulder," I said, motioning for her to toss me the bag of bite-sized. I grabbed a handful and tossed it back. Chloe heard the crinkle of the wrapper and glanced up. "Not a chance. No chocolate for you." Chloe gave me a soft snort of displeasure then went back to sleep. "Don't you think inviting him down here is a bit forward?"

"No, I don't," she said, shaking her head. "And I've always found, that early in a relationship, having the home field advantage can be very useful."

"Gee, I don't know," I said, shaking my head. "After he eats Chef Claire's food for three days, I might not be able to get rid of him. What are we going to do if I end up hating him?"

"Pack him a snack and send him on his way," Josie said, laughing. "But like I said, there's only one way to find out."

"I guess you're right. Okay, I'll give it some thought."

"Oh, that oughta help."

"Shut it."

"How do you want to handle Maria when she gets here?" Josie said, turning serious.

"I thought we'd just use the direct approach," I said. "You know, confront her with the fact that we know she's scared about something."

"And after that?"

"I'm sure I'll think of something."

"Good plan."

"I'd like to see if we can talk her into sticking around here while the Chief and I head over to the Anderson place."

"Because you don't want to put her in the middle of what might happen?" Josie said, tossing the bag of bite-sized back into the drawer. "Like getting shot."

"Yeah, there is that," I said, nodding. "And I'd hate to see her get arrested."

"You really don't think she's involved in this?"

"Not directly. I think she just got caught up in it. And now she doesn't know what to do."

"And you came up with that theory just because somebody put her dog on a paddleboard as a way to threaten her?"

"Pretty much," I said. "It's just a feeling I have that won't go away."

"Well, your gut instincts are usually right when that happens," Josie said. "So, you want to invite her to stay for dinner and a sleepover?"

"Whatever works that will keep her out of the way."

We looked at the door when we heard the knock and Sammy poked his head in.

"Maria is here to pick up her Maltese."

"That's great, Sammy," I said, gently lifting Chloe up and setting her down on the floor. "Just ask her to swing by the office so we can say hi. Go ahead and get Mellow ready, but leave her in her condo until I give you the word. And could you take Chloe with you? Just to be on the safe side."

"Are you expecting trouble?" Sammy said, turning protective as he glanced back and forth at us.

"No, I'm not," I said.

"Okay. I'll send her in."

Sammy exited, and I sat up straighter on the couch. Moments later, we heard a soft knock then Maria poked her head inside the office.

"Hi, guys," she chirped.

"Hey, Maria," I said. "Come on in."

"I suppose I've got a few minutes to chat," she said, sitting down next to me on the couch. "I love your place."

"Thanks," Josie said. "Where's your traveling companion?"

"Kirk? Oh, he was tired and decided to take a nap. It was a long trip back from Mazatlán. I'm going to meet him in a couple of hours at the hotel."

"Before you head over to the Anderson place?" Josie said.

"Yes, I can't believe he forgot that much stuff," Maria said.

"What did he forget?" I said.

"A bunch of papers and some clothes he wants back, primarily," she said, her eyes drifting off. "I think there's a set of the new board designs over there, too. And we can't have those floating around, right?"

"No, you don't want that," I said. "I guess these new designs must be pretty special."

"Yes, they are," she said, nodding with a blank stare on her face. "Julian says they're a total game changer."

"When will the new boards start showing up in that chain of surf shops?" I said, going for casual. "What's the name of those shops? JEMS?"

"Probably early next year," Maria said casually, before stopping to stare at me. "How do you know about JEMS? Are you a paddleboarder or a surfer?"

Josie stifled a snort. I shot her a dirty look before focusing on Maria.

"I just happened to come across them," I said, lying through my teeth. "Over forty stores already. That's pretty good growth for a company that's only been around a little over a year."

"Yes, their company is growing very fast," Maria said, still unable to make eye contact. "They buy a ton of product from us."

"It's essential to have a good distribution system," I said.

"Yes, it is," she whispered.

"I've never been in one of their shops," I said.

"I haven't either," Maria said. "I'm always stuck in my office doing the finance thing."

"And the shops are all located in various surf towns?"

"Pretty much," she said, slowly nodding her head. "That makes sense, right? You know, selling your products in the same places where the people are who use them."

"That makes all the sense in the world," I said. "And JEMS rapid growth is completely understandable since there are so many users of your product."

"Products. As in plural," Maria said, glancing at me.

"I'm only talking about the one," I said.

Maria flinched, then her face went blank. I waited out a silence that seemed to last forever. I eventually shifted on the couch to face her.

"How much do you know about what's going on, Maria?" I said softly.

She glanced over at me, tears welling in her eyes.

240

"Not as much as I should," she whispered.

"Whoever put Mellow on that paddleboard was sending you a message, weren't they?"

"Yes."

"A message to keep your mouth shut."

"Uh-huh," she said, nodding.

"Do you know who it was?"

"No, but I have a pretty good idea," she said, the tears now flowing.

"But you're afraid to find out, right?" I said, handing her a box of tissues.

"It's really none of my business," she said. "Like Julian says, I should just stick to doing my job and leave the rest to him."

"I would think that as the CFO of Paddles, dealing with financial irregularities would be part of your job."

"Yeah, one would think," she said, her shoulders shaking as she began sobbing.

"What do you know about JEMS?"

"Nothing really," she said, wiping her eyes with a fistful of tissues. "But a few months ago, I started seeing some numbers between them and our company that didn't make any sense."

"They were inflated on the JEMS side, weren't they?" I said.

"How on earth do you know that?" she said, giving me a wide-eyed stare.

"It's not important," I said. "And those inflated numbers were probably used as the justification for them to keep opening additional surf shops. Maybe to help them qualify for additional financing so they could grow even faster?"

"That's what I assumed," she said.

"So, you don't know who owns JEMS?" I said.

"No, I don't," she said. "I asked Julian a few questions after I saw the numbers, and he said the shops were just taking off. So, I let it go."

"Because you didn't want to rock the boat and run the risk of losing Julian or your job, right?"

I waited out a long silence.

"Yeah, that pretty much sums it up," she whispered. "I love him. And I've got millions in options riding on Paddles' success. No pun intended."

"You do know where all the money is coming from, don't you?" I said, glancing at Josie who continued to listen very closely to the conversation.

"I have my suspicions. But I don't have any proof. And neither do you," she said, nodding to herself. Then she sat up straight and placed her hands on her knees. "What's keeping Mellow?"

"Sammy is just getting her cleaned up. She'll be here in a minute."

"Good. I really need to run."

"Running probably isn't a bad option, Maria," I said, staring at her.

"What are you talking about? I'm no threat to Julian or the company."

"People do strange things when they get nervous."

"I'm not nervous," she said, wringing her hands.

"I wasn't talking about you," I said. "I don't think it's a good idea for you to go with Kirk tonight."

"Why on earth not?" she said, confused.

"Well, just off the top of my head, I can think of two very good reasons," I said. "The first is that the cops are going to be waiting for you to show up at the Anderson place."

"What? Why?"

"I think the police want to take a look at Kirk's belongings," I said.

"I see. And the other reason?"

"I have a funny feeling that somebody is going to try to kill you tonight, Maria."

"That's ridiculous," she said, managing a small laugh. "Kirk would never hurt me."

"Yeah, probably not," I said, shrugging. "But if I was faced with the choice of either being arrested or killed or eating dinner with Josie and Chef Claire, I know which one I'd take."

"But he's expecting me to go with him," Maria said.

"Just give him a call and tell him you're sick," I said. "Food poisoning is always a good excuse."

"No, I need to be there," Maria said. "Julian is expecting me to keep a close eye on Kirk."

"Because he thinks Kirk is involved in whatever is going on?" I said.

"Yes, I'm sure he does."

"Kirk and Rock. The two board designers," I said.

"Yeah," she whispered. "That's what we think."

"So, Julian isn't involved?"

"No, of course not," she said, exhaling loudly. "And why would he be? Paddles is doing great."

"That is a good question," I said, glancing at Josie who shrugged back.

"Do you really think I might be in danger?" Maria said.

"Even if you're not, there's a good chance you'll be arrested," I said. "And that would mean being locked up and separated from Mellow."

"I couldn't bear that," she said, tearing up again. "But why would I be arrested? I haven't done anything."

"Guilt by association, primarily," I said.

"And the CFO is always a target when the cops get suspicious about the financials," Josie said.

"I'm very aware of that," Maria said, her temper flaring briefly. "So, if I stay here tonight, what happens tomorrow?"

"Well, if nothing happens, you'll touch base with Kirk in the morning fully recovered from your bout with food poisoning. And if something does happen, we'll just have to see how it plays out. But either way, you and Mellow will be safe."

Maria stared off at the far wall deep in thought then slowly nodded.

"Okay," she said. "Can I go get Mellow now?"

"Absolutely," I said. "Sammy will take you back to the condos."

"And I'll meet you back there in a few minutes to take you up to the house," Josie said.

Maria glanced back and forth at us, tired and beaten down. She got to her feet and shuffled out of the office. I heard her and Sammy talking in reception then they headed toward the condos.

"What do you think?" Josie said.

"I believe her," I said. "She definitely has a good idea about what's happening, but I don't think she's involved."

"I don't either," Josie said. "But she sure has a big blind spot."

"She certainly does. And it's big enough to drive a truck through. But right now, she's scared to death her world is about to fall apart and collapse on her," I said.

"Yeah. It's too bad she's right."

"Are you sure you're comfortable keeping an eye on her?" I said. "She might do something crazy."

"No, not at all. She's scared but harmless," Josie said. "But this guy Kirk might be something else altogether. Be careful out there tonight."

"I'll be fine," I said, glancing at my watch. "The Chief and Detective Williams are going to be at the house with me. And they're going to have a bunch of cops in a police boat anchored just offshore near the house."

"Okay. But promise me *you* won't do anything crazy."

"Sure, sure."

Chapter 23

Maria had told us that Kirk was planning to arrive by boat, so Detective Williams and the Chief piled into my SUV, and we headed for Wellesley Island, crossed the bridge, and made our way to the Anderson place. I glanced through the rearview mirror at Detective Williams when we reached the apex of the bridge. He was sitting quietly peering out the window at the magnificent section of the River dotted with dozens of islands that stretched out below.

"Nice work getting your hands on all that information," I said to him, making eye contact through the mirror. "You work fast."

"Thanks," he said. "You did some good work yourself."

"Well, look at us," I said, smiling at him through the mirror. "Playing nice together in the same sandbox."

"I suppose we should enjoy it while it lasts," the detective said, resuming his stare out the window.

I parked on the side of the road a couple hundred yards from the house, and we walked the rest of the way. It was just after sunset, and the light was fading fast. Detective Williams headed down to the dock, and I waited with the Chief at the bottom of the stairs that led up to the deck.

247

"There's the police boat," the Chief said, pointing out at the water.

"Where? I can't see it," I said, squinting. "Okay. I got it now. What's that thing on the bow?"

"It's a parabolic microphone," the Chief said. "For long-range eavesdropping."

"Can they hear us now?" I said.

"I'd be very surprised if they couldn't," the Chief said. "Those things are good up to several hundred yards."

"So, I shouldn't tell any cop jokes, right?" I said, grinning.

"Probably not a good idea," the Chief said as Detective Williams returned. "Did you talk to the cops on the boat?"

"I did," the detective said. "They're all set. All we'll need to do is grab this guy Kirk. And if we get lucky, maybe he'll be in a chatty mood and save us several hours of questioning at the station."

"I can get him to talk," I said.

"Absolutely not," the Chief said.

"If he's involved in what we think he is, he won't talk to the cops. He'll just keep his mouth shut and lawyer up."

"No way, Suzy," Detective Williams said. "In fact, now that I think about it, I'd prefer if you'd just wait in the car."

"So, now I'm the chauffeur?" I snapped.

"I didn't mean to offend you, Suzy," the detective said.

"You could have fooled me."

"You've done a great job helping us get to this point," the detective continued. "But you're a civilian, and this is the part of the program where the shooting tends to start."

"He's right, Suzy. Let's not forget what happened the last time," the Chief said. "And that was just a flare gun."

I glanced around, then my neurons flared, and I rubbed my forehead. Then I glanced back and forth at them with a small smile.

"Fine. Have it your way," I said, wheeling around. "I'll be in the car."

As I walked away, I heard the Chief's voice.

"Geez, why don't I believe her?"

"I can't believe she finally listened to something I told her," the detective said. "C'mon, let's get up to the house."

I made my way back to the car, opened the back hatch, and rummaged through my bag. I grabbed a pair of night vision goggles and a flashlight. I was about to close the hatch when I paused to rummage through my bag again. I located a fresh bag of bite-sized then headed back toward the house. I worked my way around the far side of the house to stay out of sight and walked down the grassy incline toward the storage shed I'd remembered from my initial visit when

Gordo and Charlie had shown up to pick up their new paddleboards. The boards had been stored there, and if my assumptions were correct, Kirk would be more interested in what was inside the shed as opposed to anything that might be in the house. In fact, there was a good chance that Kirk wouldn't even bother going into the house. I reached the storage shed and poked my head around a corner to sneak a peek at the house. I saw the beam of a flashlight, then it disappeared, and the house went dark.

"Have a nice time waiting, guys," I whispered with a giggle as I slipped the night vision goggles over my head and tightened the strap.

I slowly pushed open the shed door and stepped inside. I closed the door behind me and checked the latch. Then I had an idea. I opened the door and examined the latch from the other side. Deciding that if I could remain out of sight outside the shed when Kirk arrived, as soon as he stepped inside, all I would need to do is secure the door from the outside and keep him trapped. But to make my plan work, I'd need a piece of rope or a chain. I closed the door and looked around the storage shed through the goggles.

Then I heard the sound of footsteps approaching. Either Kirk had turned his boat off and drifted to the dock, or I simply hadn't been paying close enough attention. Nervous sweat trickled down the back of my neck, and I looked around the shed, desperate to come up with a new plan. Two large paddleboards were leaning against the wall closest to the door. The rest of the shed contained all the usual suspects required for effective lawn and garden maintenance.

I ran my hand over one of the paddleboards as I tried to figure out my next step. I finally decided to build a hiding place behind the boards, and I bent down and grabbed one of the boards with both hands and tried to lift it. I barely got it off the ground, and I grunted and nodded to myself in the darkness, my suspicions confirmed.

"That's a lot heavier than the one we dragged out of the water."

The footsteps got closer, and I silently cursed myself for making the stupid mistake of getting trapped inside a storage shed with a man who could easily turn dangerous. My neurons surged again, this time with panic, and I glanced around for a weapon. I spotted a small garden shovel, and I gripped it with both hands. I leaned against the wall near the door with the shovel raised and my breathing rapid as I waited for Kirk's entrance. The door slowly opened, and a man stepped inside, cloaked in shadow. I screamed and took a wild swing with the shovel.

"I thought you were going to wait in-"

The shovel smacked the Chief on the shoulder, and he went down hard on the concrete floor.

"Oh, Chief. I'm so sorry," I said, dropping the shovel and kneeling down.

I closed the door and turned the flashlight on.

"What the hell do you think you're doing?" he snapped as he rolled over onto all fours.

"Defending myself?" I whispered.

"Geez, that hurts," he said, struggling to his feet. "What did you hit me with?"

"Garden shovel. Are you okay?"

"I'll live," he said, brushing himself off then checking his shoulder for damage.

"What are you doing here?" I said.

"That's funny, I was going to ask you the same question."

"We assumed that he was coming back to get something out of the house. Then I remembered this shed," I said. "I'm sure this is what Kirk is looking for."

"He's looking for the storage shed?"

"No, not the shed," I said, frowning. "He's looking for those two paddleboards. Actually, he's looking for what's inside them."

The Chief glanced at the boards, then walked over to them and lifted one a couple of inches off the ground with his good arm.

"So, you were right. Remind me to congratulate you later after I cool off," he said, then waved away the flashlight beam I was shining in his eyes.

"How much product can they fit in one of those boards?"

"Judging by the size of the board and how heavy it is, I'd say anywhere between forty to fifty kilos," he said. "I can see why they'd want them back."

"Maybe Charlie was supposed to deliver that board to somebody in the area. But then he got shot, and they forgot all about it. That's possible, right?"

"Sure, that's possible," he said, continuing to massage his shoulder. "But who shot him?"

"We'll know soon enough," I said. "Charlie must have gone rogue and was cutting his own deals, or he was starting to get cold feet and thinking about talking to the wrong people."

"Building their boards in Sinaloa was a stroke of genius," the Chief said. "Tons of drugs come through that area."

"And that's why they have that secure area in their factory," I said.

"Uh-huh," he said, nodding. "So that means Kirk and the other designer, Rock, are up to their neck in this deal."

"Yeah," I said. "So, why did you come down here?"

"We got a call from the police boat that they saw a woman walking around down here," the Chief said.

"How the heck did they see me in the dark?" I said, frowning.

"You think you're the only one with night-vision glasses?"

"Good point."

"They assumed that Maria had changed her mind and decided to show up. But I knew it was you."

"Nothing gets past you," I said, grinning.

"Yeah, that's why they pay me the big bucks," he said, glancing around. "Okay, new plan."

"I suppose you expect me to go wait in the car."

"No, I'm not going to waste my breath on that," the Chief said. "We'll wait here together. But it sure would be nice if we could get the jump on him. I'd really like to avoid a shootout."

I looked around, then noticed a shelf that ran along the wall near the door a couple of feet off the floor.

254

"Hey, I think I've got an idea," I said.

"What's that?" the Chief said, confused.

"If we open the door just a bit and rest the top of that board on it, and put the other end of the board on that shelf, with that angle, I think that board would drop like a rock when the door opens all the way."

"It would be about a three-foot drop," the Chief said, nodding. "I doubt if it would kill him, but it'll certainly get his attention. I like it."

"Okay, give me a hand," I said.

"If we're going to open the door, you better turn the flashlight off," the Chief said.

I switched it off, then opened the door about a foot.

"I can't see a thing in here," the Chief said.

Still wearing the goggles, I fumbled until I found the Chief's hand then led him to the board that was still leaning against the wall.

"If you can lift the bottom, I'll position it on top of the door," I said.

"Got it," the Chief said, letting go of my hand to grab the board.

I flinched, then whispered.

"Uh, Chief?"

"Yeah?"

"That's not the board."

"Yeah, I just figured that out. Sorry."

"Just lift the board."

He did, and I raised both arms over my head and gently positioned the board on top of the partially open door. It was perched precariously but seemed steady enough. I wiped my hands on my jeans and took a step back. Through the goggles, I saw the Chief glancing around the dark storage shed.

"Now, I guess we just wait," he said. "He should be here soon."

I noticed two wooden boxes used to transport fruit, and I set them down on their ends. We both sat down in the dark.

"Feel like making small talk?" I whispered.

"Sure, why not?" he said, laughing.

"Shhh," I said, giggling. "Oh, I almost forgot. Josie said to remind you that Wally is due for his shots."

"I think he's already scheduled for next week."

"Good. You want to go fishing this weekend?"

"Sounds great," he said. "I know there's a Muskie out there somewhere with my name on it."

"Good luck with that," I said, then grabbed his arm. "Hang on. I heard something."

"Yeah, me too," he whispered.

We listened closely to the sound of approaching footsteps. Then they stopped, and I sensed the presence of someone standing right outside the door. I forced myself to focus on my breathing and waited. I looked around through the goggles but couldn't see anyone.

"Chief? Are you in there?"

"Detective Williams?" I said.

"Suzy? I knew it," he snapped.

"Don't come in here," the Chief said, his voice rising.

"Why not?" the detective said, laughing. "You two got a little hanky-panky going on in there?"

"Don't be disgusting," I said.

"Don't open that door," the Chief said.

Unfortunately for him, Detective Williams ignored the Chief's warning. He pushed the door open, and the paddleboard dropped like a rock and landed directly on top of his head. He went down like he'd been shot and lay unconscious on the floor.

"I think we might have killed Detective Williams," I said, kneeling down next to him.

"We? It was your plan."

"Funny. Help me wake him up," I said, gently slapping the side of the detective's face.

The detective groaned then his eyelids fluttered. He looked up at me in the darkness. Through the goggles, I couldn't miss the unfocused stare in his glazed eyes.

"Mommy?"

"Not even close," I said, then glanced at the Chief. "I'm sure he's concussed." I continued to gently slap his face. "We need to get him up to the house."

We each grabbed a shoulder and helped the detective to his feet. He was wobbly but eventually managed to stand upright without falling over.

"What was it that hit me?" he said.

"Paddleboard," I said.

"That's odd, I don't remember being out on the water," he said, staggering.

"Okay, he's done for the night," I said. "Can you get him up to the house by yourself?"

"What are you going to do?"

"I'm going to wait for Kirk to show up, what else?"

"Suzy."

"I'll be fine, Chief. And there's a boatload of cops sitting a hundred yards away. Just take care of Detective Williams. And remember, he can stretch out, but don't let him fall asleep."

"All right," the Chief said, draping his good arm around the detective. "But I don't like this."

"Relax, Chief. We're just making adjustments on the fly," I said. "You should probably leave the house lights off. And since the cops are listening in, just tell them on your way up to the house what happened. If you decide to call an ambulance, ask them to leave the siren off."

"Anything else?" the Chief said, annoyed by my rapid-fire instructions.

"No, that's about it. You better get going."

"I know I'm going to regret this."

"You worry too much, Chief."

"Yeah, like that's my problem," he said, leading a very groggy Detective Williams out the door.

Since there was no way I was going to be able to get the paddleboard balanced back on top of the door by myself, I decided a new strategy was called for. But first, I needed to move the board away from the door. I knelt down and tried to lift it, then groaned loudly when my back strongly protested. I dropped to my knees and shoved the board hard with both hands, and it scraped against the cement floor as it grudgingly moved a few feet.

"Close enough," I said, getting to my feet.

Sweat was dripping into my goggles, and my knees were scraped and aching. I fought my way through a back spasm and removed the goggles. I wiped them dry with a sleeve then slid them back over my eyes. I glanced around, and out of fresh ideas and with my neurons apparently on vacation, I picked up the garden shovel and sat down on one of the fruit boxes to wait.

I spent the next ten minutes working my way through a handful of the bite-sized doing my best to calm down. My original idea to use the falling paddleboard would have worked perfectly, but I had a pretty good idea that my new one, while not nearly as creative or elegant, would also work. But I was forced to admit that the thought of getting that close to someone who would probably be more than happy to kill me did make the hairs on my neck stand up.

Then I heard the sound of a boat approaching, and I froze on the fruit box. Then I got up and listened closely with my ear against the door and heard the engine go quiet, followed by the sound of footsteps rapidly making their way across the dock. Through the goggles, I located the second paddleboard and inched my way behind it until my I was wedged against the wall. My back protested again, and I grimaced and wiggled my butt until the spasm in my lower back subsided.

The door opened, and I peeked around the edge of the paddleboard and recognized Kirk immediately. He was whistling without a care in the world, and he flipped the light switch on. He looked around and noticed the board lying near his feet, then knelt down and lifted the board with both hands and a loud grunt.

"Man, that's heavy."

He continued to grunt as he maneuvered the unwieldy board through the door. I stepped out from my hiding place, tossed my goggles aside, and grabbed the garden shovel. I stepped out of the shed and tiptoed my way through the grass, trailing him by about twenty feet. He continued to struggle with the weight of the board as he made his way down the grassy incline. Then I broke into my best lumber and quickly caught up to him. I swung the shovel hard and landed a direct shot on the back of his head. He dropped the board, then dropped to his knees, stunned. I swung the shovel again and landed another shot, this one between his shoulders. He fell forward on the grass, semi-conscious and bleeding.

"Maria?" Kirk moaned. "Is that you? What the heck did you hit me for? I'm here to help you."

"No, it's not Maria," I said, then said in a clear voice. "Just stay where you are and give me a couple of minutes."

"How the heck would I go anywhere?" Kirk said, rolling over. "I'm seeing three docks at the moment."

"I wasn't talking to you," I said, glancing down at him. "Just stay right there on your knees."

"You weren't?" he said, glancing around.

"No, I was talking to the cops," I said, nodding out at the water.

"Cops? What are they doing here?"

"The same thing I'm doing," I said. "Trying to save your life."

"You sure got a funny way of showing it," Kirk said, gently touching the lump on the back of his head then checking his hand for signs of blood.

"Just sit there quietly," I said, glancing out at the water at the boat lights that were heading our way. "They'll be here soon."

"I don't get it," he said. "You're Suzy, right?"

"Yeah."

"Why the heck did you hit me? I was just picking up a couple of boards we forgot."

"A couple of boards packed with fifty kilos," I said. "What is it? Coke or heroin?"

Kirk glanced around then looked up at the night sky, thoroughly confused. Then he made eye contact and shrugged.

"What the heck," he said. "I can always deny I ever talked to you later."

"Yes, I suppose you could try to do that," I said, nodding.

"It's both. Twenty-five kilos of each," he said softly. "How the heck did you figure it out?"

"It was a lot of things. But as soon as I figured out how you were distributing it, it all sort of fell into place."

"Hey, I don't have anything to do with those surf shops," he said. "I just make the boards."

"I know. I guess that might help you out a bit. Especially if you're willing to cut a deal. But you better be quick about it. I think Maria might beat you to the punch."

"Maria would never do that," Kirk said, blinking rapidly. "She's in love. She's a total sucker for all that crap Julian feeds her."

"She might change her mind after she hears about tonight," I said, glancing out as the boat neared the dock.

A flashlight beam coming from the boat began sweeping the shoreline then stopped on us.

263

"Kirk," a voice from the boat shouted. I recognized Rock's voice immediately. "What are you doing sitting there on the grass?"

"Trying to recover, mainly."

"What are you talking about?"

"Ask her," Kirk said, pointing a thumb back at me.

"Maria?" a different voice called out.

Julian stood up in the back of the boat. The person next to him remained sitting.

"No, Maria isn't here at the moment," I said.

"Hang on. I know that voice," Julian said. "Who are you?"

"It's me. Suzy."

"Suzy? What the heck are you doing here?" Julian said. "Where's Maria?"

"She wasn't feeling well," I said.

"And she asked you to come?" Julian said, confused.

"No, I sort of invited myself," I said. "I just had to see for myself how hard it was to carry a paddleboard filled with drugs."

"Uh-oh," Rock whispered.

"You really shouldn't have done that, Suzy," Julian said.

"Why not?"

"Because now I'm going to have to shoot you, too," Julian said.

"Sure, sure," I said, nodding. "How are you doing, Emma?"

Emma stood up in the stern.

"Hello, Suzy."

"I suppose I need to congratulate you and Julian for all the success you guys are having with the surf shops. Forty new stores in just over a year. That's pretty impressive."

"Julian," Emma said. "What the heck is going on?"

"I have no idea," he said.

"JEMS," I said. "A rather crafty combination of Julian and Emma. It's like one of those cute couple's names. Which makes perfect sense since that's exactly what you are."

"You must have a lot of time on your hands," Julian said. "Very clever of you to put all that together."

"You know, I suppose I can understand you wanting to get rid of Charlie and this guy here," I said.

"Hey, what did I ever do to you?" Kirk said, glancing up at me, annoyed.

"Sorry," I said, waving it off before refocusing on the boat. "But how could you do that to Maria?"

"Ah, poor Maria," Julian said. "She's a good kid and a whiz with the numbers. But she just doesn't have what it takes to make it in this business."

"And when she still couldn't get with the program even after you put her dog's life at risk, you decided she had to go. And since she'd been talking with Kirk, he had to go as well," I said, then spoke in a clear, loud voice. "Hang on. Just a couple more minutes."

"I'll do my best," Julian said, laughing. "But you're kind of putting us behind schedule."

"I have a few more questions," I said.

"Go ahead," Julian said.

"Julian, let's get this over with," Emma said.

"Hang on," Julian whispered. "I need to see how much she's figured out, and who she might have been talking to."

"I can get it out of her," Rock said.

"Just hold your horses," Julian said. "She's not going anywhere. She's on an island."

I was glad to hear that Julian hadn't been paying a lot of attention during the time he'd been staying at the house. While easily accessible by boat, Wellesley Island was nine miles long with tons of roads and directly connected to the mainland.

"Go ahead and ask your questions," he said.

"Charlie had set up his own deal, hadn't he?" I said.

"Yeah, Charlie just had to go and do something stupid," Julian said. "He tried to tell me that one of the boards filled with product had been stolen. Then two weeks later, he went and bought a place in Tahiti."

"That was pretty stupid," I said, shrugging.

"That's what we all thought," Emma said.

"So, who shot him?" I said.

"That would be me," Rock said, raising a rifle and pointing it at me.

"Be careful with that thing, Rock," Kirk said. "You might end up hitting me."

"That's the plan, Kirk," Rock said.

"Okay," I said, loud and clear. "I think you guys have got enough."

"What?" Julian said.

Then a floodlight illuminated their boat, and a voice boomed through a loudspeaker.

"Drop the rifle! Now!"

Rock turned his head and was stunned to see the police boat bobbing in the water about twenty feet behind them.

"Don't even think about it," the cop holding the loudspeaker said. "Or several pieces of you will be fish food."

"Yuk," I said, grimacing at the mental picture.

Rock glanced around at the four cops who had their guns pointed at him and decided he didn't like his odds. He slowly set the rifle down then raised his hands. Moments later, the police had boarded the boat and handcuffed all three. Two other police hopped out and made their way down the dock and led Kirk back to the police boat. The cop who'd been holding the loudspeaker made his way down the dock toward me.

"You had me worried for a minute there, Suzy."

"I knew you had my back, Barry. Thanks."

"No problem."

"How did you manage to get your boat that close behind them without them noticing?" I said, nodding my head in approval. "That was pretty cool."

"Well, we're good at what we do. And it is pretty dark out there," he said, laughing. "What happened to Detective Williams and the Chief? We were listening, but it was hard to follow."

"I ended up hitting the Chief with a shovel, and that board fell on Detective William's head. Did you call an ambulance?"

"No, the Chief called me when he got back to the house and said they didn't need it," he said, glancing at the house. "Speak of the devil, here they come."

I turned and saw both men slowly making their way down the path. They looked a little worn out but seemed to be okay.

"Hey," I said. "How are you feeling?"

"My shoulder's killing me," the Chief said. "And this guy must have a monster of a headache."

"You both need to get checked out. We'll swing by the hospital on the way home."

"Yeah, that's probably a good idea," the Chief said.

"Did you get it all recorded?" I said to the state policeman named Barry.

"Every word," he said. "And if this woman Maria decides to play ball, we're going to have more than enough."

"She wasn't involved," I said.

"Yeah, the CEO made that pretty clear," Barry said. "But she still might catch an accessory charge."

"But not if she cooperates, right?"

"That would certainly help her chances," he said.

"That's good," I said, nodding. "Because I'd hate to see her and Mellow get separated."

"Mellow?" he said, frowning. "Is that a family member?"

"Her dog."

The cop stared at me with a grin and shook his head.

"You are something else."

"Finally," I said, glancing back and forth at the Chief and Detective Williams. "Somebody notices."

"Well, you did good," Barry said. "Thanks again. Okay, I have several people I need to officially arrest, so I'm going to get going. And I need to make a call to the Mexican authorities."

"Oh, that's right," I said, snapping my fingers. "I almost forgot to tell you. The password to the restricted area of the factory where they build those boards is Paddles."

"It is?" the Chief said, frowning.

"Yeah, I was looking at my phone yesterday and realized that the code spells out the name of the company. It's a lot easier than trying to remember all those numbers."

"How about that? My first international case and it was solved in a day," Barry said.

"Yeah, I smell a promotion coming for you," I said.

"Me too," he said, laughing.

"What about me?" Detective Williams said.

"You expect a promotion for this? Twenty minutes ago, you were asking for your mommy."

"I was?"

"Yeah, but don't worry. I won't tell."

"Uh, Suzy. I think you just did," the Chief said.

"Oops," I said, winking at Detective Williams. "Sorry about that."

I beamed at him, then headed up the path that led back to my car.

Chapter 24

A few days later, I was sitting with Josie and my mother in the dining room at C's studying the lunch menu and making small talk until the Chief arrived. The weather had turned cold and windy, and the possibility of freezing rain had been forecast for later. Despite the weather, my spirits were high, and my neurons were quiet.

"It's a good day for soup," Josie said, scanning her menu.

"You're only going to have soup?" I said, glancing across the table at her.

"Yeah, right," she said, laughing as she flipped the page.

"Silly me," I said to my mother. "Don't forget that we're having dinner for you at the house on Friday."

"You don't have to go to all that trouble, darling," my mother said, setting her menu aside. "It's just another birthday."

"It's no big deal, Mom," I said. "And it'll be a small group. Your birthday party here on Saturday night is going to be too crowded to give you your presents, so we thought we'd do it over dinner at the house."

"Oh, I don't need anything, darling," she said, waving it away.

I glanced over at Josie who smiled then shook her head and went back to her menu.

"I hope you don't mind that I invited Paulie," I said.

"Yes, he told me," my mother said. "That was very nice of you."

"So, how was Vegas, Mrs. C.?"

"It was wonderful," she said, beaming. "I suppose you both would like to hear some of the details."

"Uh, no. That's okay, Mom. We'll just use our imagination."

"Your loss," she said, shrugging. "I think I'm going to have soup, too."

"I also invited the guy I met in Mexico," I said, casually tossing it out.

"Really? That's wonderful, darling. I can't wait to meet him."

"Just promise you'll try to go easy on him, Mom."

"What on earth are you talking about?"

"No playing twenty questions with him, and absolutely no conversations about grandkids."

"Fair enough," she said, waving at the Chief who was making his way through the dining room.

"Good afternoon, ladies," he said, sitting down and grabbing a menu. He grinned at us then scanned the lunch choices. "Great. The special is the Chateaubriand. But it serves two." He glanced at Josie. "You want to split it with me?"

"No, but she'll be happy to eat half of it after she finishes her lunch," I said, laughing.

Josie made a face at me, then tossed her menu aside.

"So, Chief, what's the update?" I said, dredging a piece of bread in olive oil.

"I just got off the phone with Detective Williams," the Chief said, accepting the bread basket I was holding out.

"How's his head?" I said.

"He's fine. He gets his stitches out in a couple of days," he said. "But he's still not happy that he missed all the action the other night."

"I'm sure he'll have lots of other chances to be a hero," I said.

"Oh, let's hope not," my mother said.

"Tell me about it," the Chief said, nodding. "But this morning, law enforcement from eight different countries launched a coordinated effort and raided all forty-one of the JEMS' shops. And the Mexican police seized control of the Paddles factory."

"And?" I said, leaning forward.

"They found boards filled with coke and heroin in over thirty of the shops, and the police are convinced that all of them are involved. Take a guess at how much product they found in that restricted area of the factory in Punta Chicado."

"You know I'm not any good at math, Chief," I said, laughing.

"Just over fifteen hundred kilos."

"Wow. That's a big number," I said, whistling softly. "Is anybody talking yet?"

"Everybody except Julian and Emma," the Chief said. "The rest of them are dying to cut their own deal."

"Kirk, too?"

"Absolutely. His story is that he was brought into the company because of his design skills and then just got caught up in things. You know, easy money and lots of it. He said he was starting to get cold feet, and he and Emma were working together trying to figure out a way to go public."

"Do the cops believe him?" Josie said, reaching for a piece of bread.

"It's mixed," the Chief said. "But even if he manages to convince them, he's still going away for a while."

"Because you can't handle that much dope and get off scot-free no matter how many people you throw under the bus?" I said.

"Exactly," he said.

"What was the deal with that guy Matisse?" I said. "Was he involved?"

"Apparently not. From what they can tell, Emma was keeping him around just to deflect attention away from the fact that she and Julian were an item. And she dropped a few hints that Julian hated the fact that Emma was always tormenting him with the idea she was seeing somebody else."

"Just to keep Julian on his toes and doing what she wanted?" I said.

"I don't know," the Chief said. "Their relationship sounds pretty strange, and neither one of them was shy about sleeping around. Maybe they were just bored. They were making more money than they could spend in ten lifetimes."

"What about Maria?" I said.

"She offered to cut a deal right after she got picked up," the Chief said. "She's doing everything she can to make sure the cops can follow the money trail."

"So, she was involved," I said, crushed.

276

"Probably not in the actual sale of the product. And she swears she didn't know it was Julian and Emma who owned the surf shops. But she definitely did her part to hide a lot of the money. She's managed to make bail and has herself a good lawyer, so I guess we'll see."

"I guess we'll just hang onto Mellow until we hear from her," I said to Josie.

"Yeah," Josie said, nodding. "And she's doing fine with us at the Inn."

"She's a lovely little dog," my mother said. "I'd be happy to look after her. And she'd fit perfectly on my lap."

"No, Mom," I said, shaking my head. "I don't think that's a good idea."

"Why on earth not?" she said, frowning.

"Well," I said, deciding to lie through my teeth. "The dog is kind of like…evidence."

Josie stifled a snort.

"Evidence?" my mother said. "Darling, are you sure you weren't the one who got hit in the head by that paddleboard?"

"It's just not a good idea, right, Chief?" I said, kicking him in the shins under the table.

"Ow. What? Oh, yeah. It's probably better that the dog stays at the Inn."

"Fine," my mother said, miffed at me.

"What I can't figure out is how the two kayakers were involved in this mess," Josie said, grabbing another piece of bread.

"I imagine they weren't happy with the new arrangement," I said.

All three of them stared at me and waited.

"My guess is that early on they were two of the primary distributors," I said. "They'd show up at one of the races with several different boards, one or more of them filled with dope. And they'd turn the boards over to the buyer and get a nice cut of the profits. But when Julian and Emma started opening all the surf shops, the demand for Charlie and Gordo's services was going down in a hurry." I glanced at the Chief. "How am I doing so far?"

"Not bad," he said, nodding.

"Julian started shipping the boards directly to the shops right from the factory, and Charlie and Gordo figured out that their window was closing. They started moonlighting and selling the boards on their own." My neurons flared briefly, and I looked over at the Chief. "Some of those surf shops had been robbed in the past several months, hadn't they?"

"You are good," the Chief said, shaking his head.

"And Julian and Emma figured out that the shops were being robbed at the same time and place a race they were sponsoring was being held. Since Gordo and Charlie always participated in their races, they put two and two together and figured out they were the ones ripping them off."

"I'm impressed, Snoopmeister," the Chief said.

"Aren't you sweet," I said, grinning at him. "But what about the two boards we found in the storage shed?"

"What about them?" the Chief said.

"Josie and I were having dinner at the Anderson place when they showed up looking for their new boards," I said.

"According to Rock's story, they did pick up new boards for the race," the Chief said. "And the original plan was for Charlie and Gordo to come back later while everybody was at the after-race party here at the restaurant and pick up the other two. But then Julian and Emma came up with the idea for Rock to take them out during the race. You know, several hundred possible suspects, and a lot of chaos on the River."

"As opposed to running the risk of leaving possible clues at the Anderson place," I said, nodding.

"Yeah, that's Rock's story."

"Why didn't he also shoot Gordo when he had the chance?" I said.

"After he took the first shot, the one that killed Charlie, Rock lost his footing in the tree and dropped the gun. By the time he managed to climb down and retrieve it, Gordo was way out of range."

"And that's when Julian and Emma came up with the plan to leave the boards behind and have Emma and Kirk come back and get them," I said.

"Yeah, diabolical, huh?"

"Good plan," I said, nodding.

"But not good enough."

"Have they found Gordo yet?"

"No, he's disappeared into the vapor," the Chief said, giving me a small smile.

"But you did just happen to mention to Detective Williams that he should probably contact the authorities in New Zealand, right?"

"Nothing gets past you."

I beamed at him and glanced up as our server approached.

"Hey, James. How are you doing?"

"I'm great, Suzy. Have you folks decided what you're going to have?"

"I'm going to start with the soup," Josie said. "But I can't decide between the French Onion or the Spinach Ham."

"If I were you, I'd go with the Spinach Ham," I said.

"Why?"

"Because it's green. And it matches your blouse."

"Good call."

Epilogue

I was in the kitchen with Chef Claire serving as her sous chef, and keeping one ear on her instructions and the other on which embarrassing childhood stories my mother was regaling Max with in the living room. So far, she'd steered clear of the most cringe-worthy, and I relaxed a bit and focused on the carrots I was julienning. I finished, put my knife down, and took a sip of wine.

"Okay, I think I'm done," I said. "How do they look?"

Chef Claire looked up from the chicken breasts she was dunking in a large bowl with both hands and glanced at the carrots. "Perfect. You're hired."

"Thanks. What's next?"

"Now, you can get started on the onions," she said, nodding at a bag on the counter. "I need four sliced wafer thin. Use the mandoline."

"I hate using that thing," I said, kneeling down to locate the device. "I'm always worried I'm going to lose a finger."

"Well, if you do, just make sure you bleed in a different direction," she said.

"I'll do my best," I said, gently punching her on the shoulder.

"Has your mom told him the story about the time you were in second grade and decided to play doctor with Jerry Adams in front of the rest of the class? That's one of my favorites."

"No, thankfully she's stayed away from that one," I said, unpeeling one of the onions.

"That's okay," Chef Claire said. "I'll tell him later."

"Don't you dare," I said, carefully positioning the onion on the mandoline. "And for the record, we weren't playing doctor. He was merely showing me how his new stethoscope worked."

"A seven-year-old with a stethoscope?" Chef Claire said, frowning.

"Yeah, he always wanted to be a doctor."

"Did he end up going to med school?"

"No, he never made it."

"What did he end up doing?"

"Fifteen to twenty for bank robbery," I said.

"At least he got to use his stethoscope on the safes, right?" she said, laughing.

"Exactly."

We both heard the knock on the kitchen door, and I answered it. Freddie and the Chief strolled in carrying bottles of wine.

"Something smells good," Freddie said.

"Hey, guys," I said, accepting the wine bottles. "Everybody's in the living room."

"Including your new guy?" the Chief said, sneaking a peek.

"Yes, he's here," I said. "So, behave yourself."

"He's staying for the weekend?" Freddie said, giving the Chief a smug smile.

"Well, since the party at the restaurant tomorrow night will probably go until at least midnight," I said, deflecting. "I really couldn't expect him to drive home after that."

"Of course not," Freddie said. "But you guys have got lots of room here."

"Yeah," the Chief said. "Plenty of spare bedrooms."

"Shut it," I said, glaring at both of them. "Now, go grab yourself something to drink, and you better hit the appetizers before they're all gone."

"Is Josie in there?" the Chief said.

"She is."

"Then we better hurry, Freddie."

"Play nice," I called after them.

I refocused on the onions, and despite my best efforts, was soon dealing with tears and burning eyes. I washed my hands then rinsed my eyes with cold water and was drying them with a clean dishtowel when I heard another knock on the door.

"That's odd," I said, heading for the door. "I thought everybody was here."

"They are," Chef Claire said, sliding a large tray of chicken into the oven.

I opened the door and found a very tentative Maria standing on the porch.

"Maria," I said, very surprised to see her standing there. "Come in."

"No, I just stopped by to pick up Mellow," she said softly. "I tried calling, but nobody answered at the Inn."

"Everybody is up here at the house," I said. "We're having a little birthday dinner for my mom. There's plenty of food if you'd like to join us."

"No, I don't think that's a good idea," she said, giving me a small, sad smile.

"Okay, then just give me a sec to grab my keys," I said, heading for the kitchen island. "I'll be right back," I said to Chef Claire.

Maria and I walked down the path that led to the back door of the Inn. I entered the security code to turn the alarm off, then opened the door and turned on the lights. The dogs came to life, and several of them bounced and barked and wagged their tails furiously. I stopped in front of the condo where the Maltese was stretched out on her bed. But when she saw Maria, she raced for the door and hopped on her back legs. I opened the door, and the dog jumped into Maria's arms. I smiled and waited for the reunion to play out.

"Somebody's happy to see her momma," I said, laughing.

"She's amazing," Maria said, hugging the Maltese.

"She's a great dog," I said, then shifted gears. "So, where are you heading?"

"I'm going to go home and stay with my folks for a while," she said. "Just until the cops and the lawyers decide what they're going to do to me."

"What does your lawyer think?"

"She's optimistic that I'll get probation," Maria said. "But who knows, right?"

"Well, you have been cooperating with them. That has to count for something."

"I sure hope so," she said, exhaling audibly.

"Have you talked with Julian?"

"No. And I'm not going to," she said, glaring into the distance. "I was such an idiot. I'm going to be left broke with a broken heart, and I'll be lucky to get a job in fast food."

"What's going to happen to Paddles?" I said.

"It's history," she said, shaking her head. "As soon as the word got out about what was going on, all our customers disappeared. And the factory was seized by the Mexican government." She glanced over at me. "Rule number one. Be very careful about who you fall in love with."

"Yeah," I said, nodding. Her comment struck a chord with me. "That's pretty good advice."

"We need to get going," Maria said, rubbing the dog's head. "Thanks again for taking such good care of Mellow. And I'm sorry we put you through all of this."

"Don't worry about it," I said. "Actually, if you guys hadn't been here for the race, things would have turned out very differently for my mom and me. Weird, huh? You know, it's like some strange hand of fate."

"Yeah, I suppose it is," she said, heading for the door. Then she stopped and turned around. "I'm usually not someone who gives advice to others, but this time I'm going to make an exception."

"Sure. Go ahead."

"Take very good care of this life you've built."

She waved and headed outside with the Maltese tucked under one arm. I locked up and reset the security alarm then watched her from the back porch until she climbed into her car and drove down the driveway. I slowly made my way up the path to the house deep in thought. I entered the kitchen just as Chef Claire was wiping down the counters.

"Is Maria gone?" Chef Claire said.

"Yeah, she just left."

"Sad story."

"Indeed," I said. "Can I ask you a question?"

"Since when do you need permission?" Chef Claire said, laughing.

"Yeah, I really need to start working on that," I said, nodding. "We've built a pretty good life here, haven't we?"

"I doubt if they come much better, Suzy. What's wrong?"

"Nothing," I said, shaking my head. "I was just thinking about something Maria said. She offered me a piece of advice."

"Okay," Chef Claire said. "But do us all a favor and don't overthink it."

"I'll see what I can do," I said, grinning.

"Good. Now, let me give you a piece of advice," Chef Claire said. "Go into the living room and spend some time with Max and see if you can make your life even better."

"That's not bad," I said, nodding as I headed into the living room.

288

A few minutes later, we were in the dining room devouring the feast that Chef Claire had put together. I briefly considered passing on seconds, but I decided that Max needed to know exactly what he was getting into when it came to my prodigious appetite. I had barely managed to set the serving spoon down before he grabbed it and helped himself to another generous serving.

"I'm going to need a nap after this," Max said, staring down at his full plate.

"Is that what we're calling it these days?" I whispered to my plate.

The Chief stifled a snort and choked on his wine.

"What did you say?" Max said, glancing over at me.

"Nothing," I said, smiling. "But I agree. A nap sounds really good."

"I love your mom," he said, sneaking a peek at my mother and Paulie who were getting cozy at the other end of the table.

"Give her time," I said, sliding a piece of chicken into my mouth.

Max laughed and reached out to brush a strand of hair away from my face. I flinched and focused on my breathing. I finished my meal in relative silence but with a contented smile fixed firmly in place.

"Okay, I'm done," Josie said, pushing her plate away. "Chef Claire that was amazing."

"And it only took you three helpings to figure that out," I said.

"Look who's talking," Josie said. "But I guess you are going to need to keep your strength up."

"Shut it," I said, turning red with embarrassment. "How about we head into the living room? We need to give you your present, Mom."

"You don't need to give me anything, darling," she said. "Except for-"

"Mom," I said, glaring at her.

"I was simply going to say except for a hug and a kiss," she said, giving me her best crocodile smile.

"All right, Mom. You win. Let's go."

Everybody followed me into the living room and sprawled out on the chairs and couches. I added another log to the fire then leaned an arm on the mantle.

"Where are all the dogs?" the Chief said, glancing around. "The place looks empty without them."

"They're downstairs in the rec room," I said. "We'll bring them up as soon as we do presents. But before we get started, we need to ask Paulie for a favor."

"You do?" Paulie said, frowning at me.

"Yes, we need you to take a few things off our hands," I said, nodding at Josie who got up and headed down the hall toward her bedroom.

"I'll see what I can do," Paulie said, confused.

Moments later, the three Labs came trotting into the living room to greet everyone. Paulie looked around the room at the dogs, then focused on me.

"I don't understand," he said.

"We've had these guys for a few months now," I said. "But having seven dogs in the house is just too much. So we thought you might be interested in taking them. I'm sure they'd love running around your farm."

"You're joking, right?" he said, reaching down to rub the chocolate lab's head.

"We'd be honored if you could take them," Josie said.

"They're beautiful," Paulie said, tearing up.

The sight of him crying over three dogs made me rethink every gangster stereotype I'd ever heard.

"That's incredibly generous of you, darling."

"He's actually doing us a favor, Mom. But we are going to require visitation rights."

"Anytime," Paulie said, draping both arms around all three Labs.

"Okay, Mom," I said, nodding at Josie. "Are you ready for your present?"

"You're going to have a hard time beating this one," she said, laughing and nodding at Paulie and the Labs.

"Yeah, maybe," I said, watching Josie again disappear down the hall. "But you need to close your eyes."

"All right, darling," she said, closing her eyes and focusing straight ahead. "But this better not be one of your gag gifts."

"I don't think you're going to find it funny, Mom," I said, laughing.

Josie returned carrying an eight-week-old King Charles puppy in her arms. The dog was brown and white with dark, soulful eyes that had made me melt every time I'd seen her since we'd picked her up from the breeder yesterday. Josie crossed the living room and gently set the puppy down on my mother's lap. My mother flinched but kept her eyes closed tight.

"Look at that," Josie said, laughing. "Perfect fit."

"Okay, Mom, open your eyes."

My mother stared down at the puppy then gently lifted it in her arms and hugged it.

"Oh, darling," my mother gushed. "She's absolutely adorable. Look at that face. She, right?"

"Yes, Mom. She's a girl. But she's going to need a name."

"I can't believe you gave me a King Charles," she said, also tearing up.

It was the third time I'd recently made her cry. But I wasn't worried about this one.

"You like her?"

"I love her," my mother said, hugging the puppy then setting her down on her lap. "How on earth did you come up with this idea?"

"Well, after we saw you with the King Charles in Cayman, we started talking about it. Then we found a breeder and the timing of the litter with your birthday worked out great."

"Thank you so much," my mother said, getting up to give all of us a long hug. "You three are too much."

"We're just glad you like her," Josie said. "And you'll need to swing by the Inn in a couple of days so I can go over a few things with you."

"I'll be there at seven on Monday morning," my mother said, again hugging the puppy.

"Good for you," Josie said, laughing. "I'll be there at nine."

"Okay, I'm going to let the bruisers out," Chef Claire said, heading for the stairs that led down to the rec room.

Moments later, all four of our dogs bounded up the stairs, said a quick hello to everyone then greeted the puppy they'd been playing with all day. Chloe stood on her hind legs, and I rubbed her head. Al and Dente both hopped up on the couch next to Chef Claire. Captain continued to tour the room before settling down next to Josie, and she gently thumped his side in perfect time with his tail that was flicking back and forth like a metronome.

"This is nice," Max said, glancing around.

"Yeah, we like it," I said, sitting down next to him on a couch.

"So, where's mine?"

"What?" I said, frowning at him.

"I don't get a dog?" he said, raising an eyebrow at me. "I'm feeling left out."

"No," I said, laughing. "Too soon. You don't get a dog yet."

"That hardly seems fair."

"I'm sure I'll come up with something."

"Uh, Suzy," Josie whispered as she leaned in close.

"Yeah?"

"Try not to overthink it."

Made in the USA
Middletown, DE
05 October 2018